DARKNESS AT DAWN

Runyan was a born survivor. He had been around the corner from three murders in prison because his survival instinct kept him from turning those corners. Those same senses now strove to warn of danger, but Runyan was ignoring them . . .

By the dim light of the window, he bent to thrust his room key into the lock. Twenty feet down the hall, in darkness his eyes could not penetrate, a fingertip slid surreptitiously across a shotgun safety catch.

*

COME MORNING

BY JOE GORES

NOVELS

A Time of Predators (1969)
   (published by Mysterious
   Press)
Dead Skip (1972)
Final Notice (1973)
Interface (1974)
Hammett (1975)
Gone, No Forwarding (1978)
Come Morning (1986)
   (published by Mysterious
   Press)

NONFICTION

Marine Salvage (1971)

ANTHOLOGIES

Honolulu, Port of Call (1974)
Tricks and Treats (1976)
   (with Bill Pronzini)

SCREENPLAYS

Interface (1974)
Deadfall (1976)
Hammett (1977–8)
Paper Crimes (1978)
Paradise Road (1978)
Fallen Angel (1981)
Cover Story (1984–5)
   (with Kevin Wade)

TELEPLAYS

Golden Gate Memorial (1978)
   (4-hr miniseries)
High Risk (1985)
   (with Brian Garfield)
Episodic TV (1974–85):
   *Kojak; Eischied; Kate Loves a
   Mystery; The Gangster Chron-
   icles; Strike Force; Magnum,
   P.I.; Remington Steele; Scene
   of the Crime; Eye to Eye; Hell
   Town; T. J. Hooker*

COME MORNING

JOE GORES

THE MYSTERIOUS PRESS • New York

this book is for
DORI
my wife, my lover,
my best friend,
the still point of
my turning world

MYSTERIOUS PRESS EDITION

Copyright © 1986 by Joe Gores

Mysterious Press books are published in association with
Warner Books, Inc.
666 Fifth Avenue
New York, N.Y. 10103
A Warner Communications Company

Printed in the United States of America

Originally published in hardcover by Mysterious Press.
First Mysterious Press Paperback Printing: March, 1987

10 9 8 7 6 5 4 3 2 1

ACKNOWLEDGMENTS

This novel could not have been written without the generous assistance of the following people, who were remarkably selfless with their time, enthusiasm, and expertise:

Albert F. Nussbaum, for details of penitentiary life, for insights into a prisoner's feeling upon his release from captivity, and for technical data on safes and strongboxes.

Tim Gould, for detailed descriptions of rock-climbing and the equipment used in mountaineering, as well as evocations of Monday Morning Slab and the Royal Arches from a climber's perspective.

Anthony Newland, Public Information Office, California Department of Corrections, San Quentin Prison, for a no-holds-barred entree to San Quentin, and for a minute-by-minute walk-through of the prisoner release process at the prison.

Richard Creighton of Drake High School, for vetting certain portions of the manuscript and for nuances of the Spanish language not available elsewhere.

Sidney Daniels of Granat Brothers Jewelers for details concerning the fenced value and probable appreciation of stolen diamonds over a number of years.

Finally, but most especially, my wife, Dori Gores, for countless hours of work on the manuscript, from expert editorial revision and suggestion to substantive changes which gave the novel much of its present form, meaning, and humanity.

CHAPTER 1

It was raining in Portland. It was always raining in Portland, thought Big Art Elliott, unless Mt. St. Helens was dumping her crap in the streets. And sometimes even then. He jumped out of the Caddy Seville with its tucked-under tail—he always thought of a hound dog getting its butt kicked—and dodged through the rain into the branch post office. He was built like a bear, with features too juvenile for his jowly face. Only pale watchful eyes suggested his 41 years.

A local newspaper headline in the lobby coin box caught his eye: UNION OFFICIAL SUBPOENAED IN PENSION FUND PROBE. Yeah, tell us about it, he thought sourly. He had pushed a big rig for 14 years, he could give the fucking newspapers a few scoops himself.

He'd moved to an inside job four years before, and his clothes showed it: roll-collar ivory shirt open three buttons, gold medallion glinting on his hairy chest, stacked-heel over-the-ankle boots to add three inches to his six-one.

There was a letter from Runyan in his box. Christ, Runyan!

He stood at one of the tables reading it, water glinting in his thick curly brown hair and spotting the shoulders of his pinch-waist powder-blue sports jacket.

> Dear Art,
>   I figured that if none of you ever heard from me again, it would be too soon. But here I am, right where Dolly and Ma and Sissy—maybe even you— always thought I'd end up. Prison.

State? Federal? Runyan, though his younger brother, had raised all sorts of hell after Pops had died, and had gone to Nam just to stay out of the Oregon state pen.

> I'll be getting out in six weeks, and I'd like to see all of you again. If you don't want me to, just write and say so . . .

Say if anyone wanted to see him again was what he meant, though he didn't say it. Ma. Sissy. Dolly.

Dolly, Art's busted marriage. Come home from a week on the road, ready for a good steak, a good screw, and 12 hours of sacktime, what'd he get? This is broke, that is broke, we need this, we need that . . . So he got off the road, and when she found out he'd gotten a little something on the side—hell, what man wouldn't, given the chance?—she'd just walked off. With damn near everything he owned.

Art looked out into the rain, remembering, considering.

Of course during his seven years at San Quentin, Runyan had considered what it would be like to have visitors, everyone in the joint did. The call on the loudspeaker, the trek across the yard, the familiar face, the welcome smile. But his first had been only three months ago, with a call to the prison library where he made three dollars a day as a clerk.

He had barely entered the unfamiliar visitors' room when a voice had called his name.

"Runyan. In here."

In one of the meshed cages, usually used by attorneys for conferences with their clients during visitors' hours, had been an unremarkable mid-forties man, with a smart jaded face for which the world no longer held surprises. His voice had been half-drowned in the multilingual, multiracial babble, edged with hysteria, of people trying to squeeze years into minutes.

"David Moyers, investigator for Homelife General Insurance. We carried the insurance on those stones you lifted, Runyan. I'm going to bat with the parole board and I'm going to get you out. A simple thank you will do."

"Which stones are those?" Runyan had asked.

"Yeah, they told me you were a hardnose. Never admitted taking them, though they had you cold. Okay. I *know* you have them stashed, Runyan. Everyone else *thinks* you do, but I *know*. I also know you're going to deal. You might not think it now, but you will. I'm your ticket out of here."

That had been three months ago. Since then, Moyers playing him, him playing Moyers. If he dealt the stones away before he got out, he never would. But until he was out, he couldn't know for *sure* whether he *could* deal with Moyers. So he led him on, fended him off, kept him interested, and it had worked: His parole had come through and here he was, five days and a get-up before release.

But who was it today? Couldn't be Moyers; they'd talked just two days ago. Unless he was getting as edgy as Runyan was at the days marching inexorably to release date. Could that woman journalist have come back? The one who'd gotten a pass to come interview him for some book she was writing about ex-cons? He hadn't gone to meet her on the day she had shown up.

At the visitors' room he showed his I.D. and went through into the cold narrow room where prisoners were strip-searched before and after their visits.

"Okay Runyan, bend and spread 'em."

Dressed again, he was let through into the long crowded visitors' room. Instant bedlam, a terrific assault on prison-blanded senses.

Runyan checked out the attorneys' cages; no Moyers. He went all the way down the room through the throng, past the thick glass partitions where attorneys or friends could drop their ducats in the chute to talk with hard-timers from max security behind the glass. Still no Moyers.

He suddenly realized he hated visiting days: They showed you just how much you had deteriorated in the joint. A child crying in the playpen area was enough to prevent you from holding a train of thought. In the joint, things came at you one at a time. When the lights went out, the lights were out. You got beef on Wednesday, chicken on Sunday, a movie on Friday night.

But if he couldn't handle even this much change, how could he make it on the outside?

Suddenly up in front of him popped a big man in clothes a North Oakland pimp would have found gaudy. The man grabbed Runyan's hand and started shaking it while Runyan just gaped.

"For Chrissake, *Art*! I didn't expect ... You didn't have to ..."

He'd almost forgotten he'd written Art, it had been right after he'd heard he was going to be paroled, he'd had to touch someone, anyone on the outside to make it real inside himself. But here was Art, grinning like a fool. The 30 pounds he'd picked up since Runyan had seen him last had given him a sleek seal look, softening his features and eroding the cut granite edges of his hard, blocky body. But by God, he still looked like a truck driver. Probably was.

"I was going to write," said Art, "but then I thought that after eight, nine years ... all the changes ..."

Runyan dragged him over to a table being vacated in front

of the vending machines lining one wall. A tall, sad-looking black prisoner with three kids fed in coins for candy bars.

Art went on, "See, Sissy got herself married after . . . got herself married and moved to Idaho . . . Isn't easy for her to get back . . ."

"After what?"

Art ignored this. "And then Dolly, she found out I had a little something going on the side, and—"

"That wouldn't be the first time," said Runyan.

Art grinned his big sheepish grin. "But it was the last. She just fucking up and divorced me, Runyan, took everything except the house."

Runyan laughed and clapped his hands, once.

"No way Ma'd let her take that."

Art cleared his throat and looked down at his big truck driver's paws. And Runyan, even though there'd been no voice calling, My son, My son, wind-blown through his sleep, knew exactly what Art was going to say.

"Shit, there ain't any easy way. Ma died three years ago."

Runyan drew a deep shuddering breath and made a vague gesture. "I should have known, when she didn't write or anything after I sent that letter to you . . ."

Art was abruptly loud and blustery, as he always was when he didn't quite know what to say or do.

"Don't get the idea that you aren't welcome when you get out. I mean it, now. I'm not pushing a rig any more, I've got a desk job at the union . . ." He slapped the roll of belly over his trousers top. "You're looking in great shape, but I'm just getting hog fat." He stood up abruptly. "I've got the old homestead and an apartment downtown Portland, lots of room, you need money, a ticket, anything, you just call . . ."

Runyan went back for his strip search. His mother was dead and his sister didn't want to see him and Art's offer, while genuine enough, was more family than feeling. They'd never been close, Art was a talker and Runyan was a doer. Art had the strength and the size, but not the craziness.

Art hadn't ended up in the joint, either. And San Quentin's endless hours of empty routine, strictly observed, had leached away most of Runyan's craziness, too. Now all he wanted was OUT. And once he knew nothing was coming at him outside, he'd deal the diamonds away to Moyers and walk free.

CHAPTER 2

In his dream, Runyan was always dressed in black, watching the second hand of his watch climb to 12. At two a.m. precisely, he thumbed the brass latch of the loading door and pushed. No alarms went off. He slipped through, letting it ease shut behind him with a scarcely audible click.

Jamie Cardwell was already taking his key out of the alarm reset beside the door as Runyan came through; he was Runyan's age, 30, but bulkier and slower in his guard's uniform with the Sam Browne belt and holster. Runyan grinned silently at him; a line of sweat stood on Jamie's full upper lip. Runyan started up the fire stairs as Cardwell continued down the hall only 18 seconds behind his ideal patrol schedule.

Runyan eased open the heavy metal fire door on Seven and gave a quick look up and down the deserted corridor. Five minutes before the other guard's round. The key Cardwell had given him unlocked the opaque glass door of Suite 729. Thick wires were criss-crossed in glass which bore the legend:

Joe Gores

HIRAM & GATIAN SHERIDAN
GEMSTONES
Wholesale Only

Inside, he leaned against the door for a moment, having trouble breathing, with a heightened pulse and difficulty swallowing. He'd never worked with an inside man before; the adrenaline was really pumping.

Light from the street showed a lapidarian litter: hot box, small gemstone cleaner, polishing and grinding wheels, an oxyacetylene torch. Across the room, the squat old-fashioned floor safe behind the heavy wooden desk which must have last seen varnish in the 'thirties.

Just over three minutes left. Runyan began jerking out desk drawers and dumping them on the floor. The last one he carried empty to the window, where he used street light to letter R12-L10-R21-L6-R13 on the back with a felt-tipped marking pen. He dropped this drawer also, then waited. Right on time the uniformed shadow loomed up against the glass, the knob rattled, then the shadow and footsteps moved on.

He switched on the desk lamp, directed its light at the dial of the safe, then worked the same combination he had written on the back of the drawer. He jerked the handle to one side and swung back the ponderous door. After wiping sweat from his forehead with the tennis band on his wrist, he removed the velvet-lined trays. Those with unset gemstones he emptied into a black velvet bag taken from his pocket; the others he dumped on the floor.

The slim attaché case beside the desk was a better way than his pocket to carry a couple of mil in uncut stones, so he put the velvet bag into it, left the light on and the safe gaping. Out in the hall, he took a short steel prybar out from under his sweater and jimmied open the door with it, leaving white splinters of wood around the jamb. He tossed in the prybar and left.

In the basement he crossed to the loading door, making an

8

OK circle of thumb and forefinger to Jamie, grinning like an idiot. Despite his doubts it had gone like glass; he'd been inside just 17 minutes . . .

It was at this point that Runyan always realized he was having a nightmare. Because Jamie's hand was coming up, not with the key to switch off the alarm, but with the snub-nose .38 from his already unflapped holster. There was terror in Jamie's face but murder in his hand.

Runyan, by reflex, was already swinging the attaché case, already slamming his body up against the loading door release bar. The case knocked the gun aside for the first shot; as he went through the door, the alarm started clanging and Cardwell put the second round in his back.

Runyan yelled and arched away from the tremendous thudding blow of the slug, shredding a knee painfully on the cinderblock wall of his cell. Old-timers said a horny con could circumcise himself just by rolling over in his sleep.

He lay in the bunk for a few moments, panting, then swung his feet to the concrete floor, staggered to the sink, and splashed icy water on his face in the dark. His cell was one of the relatively few singles left in Q.

The eight-year-old memory had started recurring as a nightmare when his release date had been fixed. Had some inner mechanism suspended at 15-to-life begun operating again when he made parole? The organism preparing for change, getting ready for life on the outside? Ever since he'd been short, he'd had the feeling that somebody or something was out to get him, him personally, just *because* he was short. Not other prisoners: the system, the bureaucratic process, the impersonal finger.

Short? Christ, today was the day. *Today.* This day, this morning! He rested a forearm against the bars, pressed his forehead against it; corridor light laid vertical strips of shadow down his naked muscular body. His face felt as clenched as his fist. *Today.*

After nearly a minute, Runyan turned and in the dim light

stared around the tiny stripped cell to which he had given seven years of his life. What did he really want, outside?

Was just to *be* outside enough?

No. He had to make sure he never came back here again, no matter what or who was waiting for him out there.

CHAPTER 3

Louise Graham examined her carefully wrought image in the motel room mirror. Recalling the Oscar Wilde character with the epigraph, *she had a long 29*, Louise shoved an impatient hand into her cold cream and smeared it all over her face to wipe out 20 minutes of makeup. Men were always telling her she was beautiful, but now, at 29, she couldn't see it.

The narrow oval face had too strong a chin and faint permanent laugh lines at the corners of a mouth a shade too generous. Straight narrow nose, but too much flare at the nostrils. Good brow, though, and if she did say so herself, great eyes. A sensual face: She'd always known she looked like a great lay, but beautiful, no. Sophia Loren, that was beautiful. At 90 that woman would be beautiful.

Louise impatiently jerked back her shoulder-length black hair, tightly, severely, and flicked around two turns of elastic to keep it that way. There. Better. Add a pink man-tailored blouse and grey two-piece suit with grey pumps, big round sunglasses to mask the stunning almond-shaped emerald eyes, and she was ready. Repressed sexuality, all the fires banked, all the appetites controlled, that was the look for a surly, dangerous, angry man who hadn't touched a woman in eight years.

Nor answered her letter, nor come to the visiting room on the day she'd suggested. She checked her watch. No other chance to catch him so vulnerable as today, when he emerged from San Quentin like butterfly from chrysalis, tender and fluttery and unprepared for the world into which he was being reborn.

Louise was halfway out the door when she stopped, went back, and shoved the pages of manuscript into an unlabeled manila folder. The story, written last night when she couldn't sleep, was the first fiction she'd tried in six or seven years.

Apart from letters to her folks, of course.

When the automatic lock bar at the top of his cell door slid back, Runyan rolled, fully clothed, off his bunk for the last time. His cell was stripped except for him and his clothes; the day before he'd given away all the makeshift possessions which had crowded it, and the curtains, pieced together from fabric scraps scrounged from the upholstery shop, which had shielded him from the corridor. His shaving gear and the miniature chess set carved in the woodworking shop would be waiting with his civvies at Processing.

He had observed one other ritual the day before: flashing the ace from a deck of cards as he moved about, to let others know he had one day left. Turning the knife in those remaining, as it had been turned in him scores of times. At the same time giving a little hope—if *he* can make it, so can I.

He crossed the lower yard through weak morning sunshine to Processing—despair on the way in, hope on the way out. Seven years before he had been herded in here from a bus at gunpoint; only a prisoner who had served out his time, or made parole, could walk out. Everyone else rode—in a bus or a meat wagon.

"Runyan," he told the guard at the door.

The man had the cheery russet-tinged face of a beer drinker, but the face was totally without animation.

"I.D." Runyan handed him the heat-sealed plastic yellow card with his name, face, and prison number on it. "Inside and strip."

The clothes Runyan stepped into were seven years out of date, but that was all right; so was he. It was like running a film backwards, a film which had lain in the vault unchanged for seven years while the world unrolled around it.

Accompanied by a guard, carrying his sheaf of release papers and his old yellow gym bag, he walked across the upper yard. Bright with grass and plantings, it might have been the plaza in some old California Mission town—except for the guard runway above, garnished with coils of barbed wire to discourage those hoping to leave on their own.

Getting closer to the outside skin of the prison was like coming up from a deep dive, the gloom around you turning progressively lighter, more delicate shades, as more and more sun filtered through, until you burst out with a huge WHOOSH of spent air. The final door was massive steel with iron latticework gates which could be clapped shut in case of a break.

One more check-out between him and the East Gate, beyond which the clock of time would start again. Here, no one was friendly, no one was hostile. They did this every day; Runyan would do it only once.

"Your check-out order, please."

Runyan handed the cheery-faced woman guard his papers as a Chicano prisoner drove a prison bus up to the high chain-link gate. She put the papers aside.

"Wait here a minute, I got to shake down this bus."

Runyan's escort pawed through his gym bag while she looked inside the bus and into its engine compartment; the driver stood for her quick body frisk with his arms wide and his legs slightly apart, a blank look on his face. She came back and Runyan emptied his nearly empty pockets so she could shepherd him through the metal detector. It squealed.

"The zipper on your windbreaker."

He removed the jacket and passed the detector. To his amazement, she suddenly grinned at him.

"Right down to the gate. And good luck."

He thanked her. He and his escort went down the sidewalk toward the final gate a football field away. Outside the open motor-pool building, a radio blared as a couple of prisoners hosed down a truck. To the right, beyond the fenced visitors' parking lot, raucous seagulls dipped and turned over the sparkling water of Richardson Bay.

At the gate building was a door marked THIS WAY OUT, FOLKS, but the guard blocked Runyan's passage.

"Prisoners use the gate."

It was of six-foot-high, black-iron pickets, one side opened inward. A taut, well-conditioned, hard-faced guard brought a clipboard out of the guardroom beside it.

"Name."

"Runyan."

"Check-out order and I.D."

Runyan handed over the precious warden's release order and, for the last time, his prison I.D. The guard made a checkmark on a mimeo'd sheet on his clipboard.

"You're clear, mister."

Feeling light-headed, Runyan walked through the gate with his escort. No sirens sounded, no alarms rang. The guard stopped a dozen feet beyond the gate and handed him an envelope.

"Count it, then sign the receipt."

He did. One hundred dollars.

"You'll get another hundred from your parole officer when you report. The date, time and place are on your release papers." He hesitated, then added in a different voice, "If you need transport to town, that little yellow house beyond the post office—with the sun painted on the front—that's Catholic Social Services. They can help you there."

"Thanks," said Runyan, but the guard had already turned away, as if somebody else had been using his voice.

Runyan didn't want transport to town. He wanted to walk forever down the narrow uneven blacktop, stuffing his lungs with free air as sharp as ammonia. He heard a car engine start up behind him in the lot outside the prison gate, but he didn't turn. Through his mind was running the old Pete Chatman blues number, *Gone to Memphis*.

I'm a bitter weed, I'm a bad seed,

Come morning I'll be gone.

Only it was *this* morning, and Runyan was gone away from here. To his left the hillside slanted up sharply, crowded with old frame houses in peeling, weather-beaten pastels. To his right, below road level, was a quarter-circle of new condos made out of grey-painted wood and with the plantings not yet in except for a couple of FOR SALE signs.

Who the hell would want to buy a place within eyeshot of this sprawling miserable dragon with over 3,000 dead men living in its distended gut? Apparently somebody did; a new Continental was parked in the turn-around and a burly man with black curly hair had his hands cupped against a ground-floor window.

Runyan, swinging his gym bag like a kid let out of school early, moved off to the shoulder as the car from the prison lot came up behind him. Then his neck went rigid and sweat popped out under his arms. The car was pacing him. He'd known it: It was all a macabre joke, at the last second they were going to take it all away from him.

"Runyan?"

A woman's voice. He didn't turn, but relief washed over him. They wouldn't send a woman to take him back.

"I'm Louise Graham? I wrote to you?"

He shot a quick look. Blue car, Lynx, wasn't that a Mercury?

Her window down and her face peering out from behind huge round sunglasses. Mid, maybe late twenties. Hair pulled back severely. He kept walking.

"I'm a journalist? Researching a book?"

Every phrase a question. She *sounded* like a writer, *looked* like a writer—or what he thought a writer looked like.

"You didn't answer my letter? Didn't see me on visiting day?"

Three minutes out, he was suddenly being forced to do things he hadn't needed to do in seven years. Think. Weigh. Judge. Make decisions. Act.

He kept walking.

The car shot forward and slammed to a stop in front of him, blocking his way. He glanced back involuntarily; thank God, they were out of sight of the prison gates. She stuck an angry head out the window.

"Damn you, all I'm doing is offering you a ride."

He was proud of the way his voice reflected nothing at all. "Sure you are," he said.

"Shit," said Angelo Tenconi aloud when Runyan got into the Mercury Lynx.

Tenconi was a big black-haired man with an angry jaw—blurred now by easy living—that would always need a shave. He whispered the Connie around the little turn-around and up onto the narrow blacktop. The freaking FOR SALE condos had been a good place to watch the two-million bucks leave Q, but who was the freaking broad had just picked up Runyan?

Looked like a U-Drive, maybe, but anyone coming into this would be local, was he not right? Unless, of course, they'd imported some hotshot out-of-town broad to work on him. Or maybe she was some quiff Runyan had been banging before he went away?

He drifted the Connie along three cars behind as she took the underpass up onto Cal 17 westbound. He adjusted the

16

strap constricting his chest like an auto safety belt. It was the shoulder holster for Tenconi's Smith & Wesson .41 Magnum, built on the .44 Magnum frame with the four-inch barrel.

It could shoot through a freaking engine block, it could sure as hell shoot through Runyan if it had to.

CHAPTER 4

As she drove down Waldo Grade toward the tunnel on US 101, Louise wondered how you got through to a clod like Runyan. He was handsome enough, with air from the open window ruffling his shiny black prison-chopped hair, and his eyes a piercing blue under dark even brows. But he was reacting to her as to a rock lying alongside the highway. None of her research on him ranging back to childhood had prepared her for this zombie. Could seven years in prison have turned him into a homosexual?

Well, how about vulnerability? Expose her throat, like a she-wolf showing submission to the pack's dominant male?

"Um . . . in my letter, I mentioned I was a journalist researching a book? I was working for a newspaper in Minneapolis, but I felt the need for an in-depth study of the ex-convict reentering society after a long hiatus . . ." No reaction. Didn't know the big words? "What I mean is, what happens when you hit the street after being away for a long time?"

No answer. Beyond Waldo Tunnel, San Francisco sprang up

like an enchanted city in a pop-up book of her childhood. They swept down and out onto the Golden Gate past the stunning rocky Marin headlands flanking the span.

"What I'm concerned with here are the difficulties the emerging mainline prisoner encounters in adjusting to this . . . um . . . new and bewildering complex of inputs . . ."

Nothing. Maybe he had a dead battery or something. Her voice had an edge, she couldn't help it.

"Instead of complex of inputs, how does everything coming at you at once grab you?"

Runyan finally looked over at her, making his eyes go dull. "They put saltpeter in our soup to keep our sex drive low," he said. "It makes you all mushy in the head." In the same tone, he added, "I have to report to my parole officer, if you could drop me at a bus stop on Van Ness . . ."

"I'll drive you," she said quickly.

Dammit, girl, keep the asperity out of your voice. Asperity is not what this man needs right now. Maybe she should have worn a Playboy bunny outfit instead of doing her skun rat impression. Maybe she should just *ask* him what he was thinking. Maybe she should just tell him what *she* was thinking.

I think you're a lout and a boor and a wise-ass and probably a fag, and I want you to tell me all about yourself.

Sure.

The San Francisco Parole Office was supposed to have been relocated to a nondescript two-story stucco office building between a parking lot and an old Queen Anne Victorian on South Van Ness. But the doorway was half-blocked by a pile of sand wearing a highway warning flasher with ROAD-WORK—DRIVE CAREFULLY stenciled on it. The signs on the ground floor government-funded mental health clinic and counselling service for the elderly were in Spanish only.

Runyan was checking his release papers, obviously confused.

"Could it be on the second floor?" Louise asked almost timidly; she didn't want to come on all assertive, in case he was macho man after all.

"Sure, you're right, that's it. Thanks." He opened the door and started to get out, gym bag in hand.

"You don't lose me that easily," she said. "I'll wait."

He shrugged and tossed the gym bag back in the car, as if it didn't matter much. Short brown people with broad Peruvian faces and excitable Latin discourse crowded the street. A pair of lovers passed, hand-in-hand, heads together, giggling; to Louise it was a rough-looking neighborhood, but to them it was safe territory.

Runyan pulled open the door on the curb side and began, "Look, Miss Graham, I can make it on my own from—"

"Ms. And I'm trying to interview you, remember?"

He shrugged again and got in. She drove in on South Van Ness to the broad arterial slash of Market Street; beyond rose pompous, self-important grey government buildings. As they passed the glittering Marion Davies Concert Hall, Runyan craned around in his seat, then settled back shaking his head.

"You don't like it?" she asked quickly.

"I *love* it," he said, hitting love with a hammer. "If you could turn right at Golden Gate . . ."

They went by the hulking stone Federal Building and Federal Courthouse, a grey monstrosity taking up an entire block behind a plaza that looked too sterile even to attract pigeons.

"Is this where your trial was held?"

"This is federal, I was state," said Runyan tonelessly.

How adroitly you elicit his views on things, Louise thought. First Davies Hall, then this. Maybe you ought to try to sell him magazine subscriptions. But it wasn't just her; there was some tension in him that was beyond the moment. Something having nothing to do with her, or having to do with her in a way she didn't yet understand.

The neighborhood had changed again. They were in the

Tenderloin, low life in a high crime area. Even the women looked like muggers. At the corner of Larkin the light held them as two mounted policemen clopped by, one with a huge pink carnation stuck through the mane of his sleek, wise-looking horse.

"When do you start asking me about the diamonds?" Runyan demanded abruptly.

"I don't know anything about any diamonds—other than you allegedly took a bunch of them." She strove to keep shrewishness out of her voice. "I still would have been in college when you did that, anyway."

The red light had stopped them in front of the old, genteelly seedy YMCA, with its chipping paint and earnest sign, MEN AND WOMEN—ROOMS—FITNESS CENTER.

"We don't talk about the diamonds, we don't talk," said Runyan.

Louise made an elaborately courteous gesture. "Then by all means, let us talk about the diamonds."

The light was changing; Runyan opened his door and stepped out with his gym bag.

"I don't talk about the diamonds," he said.

He walked around the corner and was gone. Louise whipped off her dark glasses to glare after him, then belatedly shot the Lynx around the corner too as the cars behind her started to honk. Runyan was half-a-block ahead, walking rapidly. On the corner two bearded men in their early thirties were kissing, hands on one another's hips.

The anger abruptly left her face. Seeing them, she knew that Runyan hadn't gone that route in prison. Which meant he was accessible to a woman in ways that Louise knew all about.

The blue sign at 531 Leavenworth still read WESTWARD HO-TEL in white letters with broken bits of neon tube dangling from them. He had roomed there once, years before, it was the logical place to list as his address with the parole authority.

Plastered beside the brown double doors at the head of the terrazzo steps were various stern warnings on pastel sheets of stiff art paper: NO SITTING ON STEPS (blue); PLEASE KEEP DOORWAY CLEAN (pink); NO VISITORS (yellow); and NO TRESPASSING (red and black). Posted off to one side was one of much heavier caliber, a dated DEMOLITION ORDER APPEAL HEARING.

He paid the pallid rat-faced clerk a week in advance on a room that was second floor back, at the far end of the cross hall next to the fire escape window. It was what you could expect in the Tenderloin for $50 a week: shabby chest of drawers, a sink in the corner with a thin napless towel on the rack, no soap or washcloth, a small hand mirror tacked above the sink partially to mask the brown water stains of an old overflow from the sink upstairs. The single bed had a human-shaped depression in the middle of it.

On the other hand, with the brown roller shade up, sunlight came through the frayed imitation lace curtains to give it a certain spurious golden charm. And it was a room, not a cell; no electrically controlled bar would slide across the door at night to keep him in.

Runyan tossed his gym bag on the dresser and stripped off his shirt. He started to run cold water into the sink to wash away the stink of Q, a need more psychological than physical.

Would she show up again? He'd detected real beauty behind those dark glasses and severe hair, but he couldn't afford the luxury of believing that she was just a writer after material.

As the sink filled, he thought, On the other hand, who would she belong to? Moyers didn't need a plant, he knew Runyan probably would turn the diamonds back to him, eventually, for the recovery fee. Unless he had become more rather than less of a man during the past seven years, Card-well wouldn't have the guts. There weren't any other players—unless, and this was his real fear, Jamie'd had partners in the betrayal . . .

But anybody smart enough to preserve his safety through eight long years of silence was too smart to put himself into the hands of a hired woman. So maybe she was what she said she was.

As he came up whooshing from the cold water, the mirror showed him Louise just coming through the door. He said immediately, without turning, "The insurance company is waiting for me to be a good little doggie and dig up their bone for them." Blinking, he groped for the towel. "They figure I have the diamonds stashed somewhere."

She had shut the door and was turning in a complete circle, taking in the room.

"It's *you*," she said.

Using the towel was like drying off with a cardboard shirt backing. She was pulling down the window shade, making the room a dim cavern where anything might happen. She tossed her sunglasses on the dresser and started shaking out her hair: Her eyes were the most beautiful Runyan had ever seen, wide-set emerald chips glowing with an inner light. He felt an involuntary thickening in the groin, a tightness in the chest, a growing wildness in his mind.

"At that college, didn't they teach you about leaving the door open when you're alone in a room with a man?"

"We had coed dorms."

She pulled out her blouse and started unbuttoning it. Oh Jesus, eight years. He almost ran to open the door, but she stepped right into him, so her face was only inches from his. Through the gauzy bra her already hardening nipples were like tiny hot coals against his naked chest. His arms came up to encircle her. Her hips were shifting against him, bringing him completely erect.

"This . . . is as far as we can take it and still quit easy," he said in a harsh voice.

"I didn't come here to quit," she said.

23

Her tongue, tasting very faintly of cinnamon, was hot between his lips. Her buttocks were taut beneath his clutching hands as he lifted her toward the bed with a cresting, almost frenzied urgency.

CHAPTER 5

The three-sided air shaft held trash cans and opened out into the alley. Runyan dropped the edge of the shade and turned back into the dimness of the room, naked. He had a gymnast's finely muscled body. Louise was pulling the wisp of bra up against her ripe, beautifully shaped breasts.

"Uh ... I'm sorry I ... uh ... started out so rough," he said. "At first I was afraid that after all this time I might be impotent. Then I just ..."

She straightened, buckling the bra, then pulled on her blouse. She winked bawdily at him. "After eight years, you're entitled to poke a little fun."

Runyan felt an unexpected surge of sad anger. This had been the fulfillment of every sexual fantasy through seven years of endless nights, and she was acting as if ...

"What *was* this for you? Kicks? Tease the animals?"

There was a hint of wicked laughter in her voice. "I did more than *tease* the animal. And—"

"What are you after?" He had grabbed her shoulders and

was shaking her, all his doubts rushing back. *"What do you want?"*

She didn't try to break free; she seemed used to coping with men to whom violence came easily.

"What do *you* want?"

Runyan's hands dropped away. He said in a low, angry voice, "I don't want to go back inside. I don't want you yelling rape unless I talk to you about the diamonds. I don't want—"

"But want do you *want?*"

He responded with silence; he had no more answer for her than he had for himself. She turned away with an abrupt briskness that made the last hours just another prison-born fantasy, picked up her purse and sunglasses and walked right out of the room without a backward glance.

"Hey!" yelped Runyan, stunned.

He started to follow her, then realized that he was naked. He turned back to snatch up his pants.

The door at the foot of the stairs swept away her reflected image as she went through it: cool, self-contained, sure of herself, almost haughty. Only she had to lean against the front of the building for a moment, she felt so shaky inside.

She started walking, buffeted by inner gales. A Chinese youth wearing a white gauze mask against pollution was unloading canned goods for the grocery store next door. A heavy-faced white man's eyes gleamed greedily at her from between the stems of a split-leaf philodendron in the window of the Chinese restaurant on the corner. In the parking lot the attendant stripped her with his eyes as he took her money and got the Lynx.

She was shaking so hard she could hardly get the key into the ignition. Her arms ached where Runyan had gripped them. She'd meant to control the situation, control him, control herself; instead, she had seduced herself with his vulnerability. She'd remembered him walking away from the prison like a jaunty, scared little kid, and all of a sudden she'd been out of control, hung out on the cruel edge of passion where she couldn't get down and it had just kept happening until it almost hurt . . .

The memory caused a slight involuntary contraction in her pelvis, as if marking the onset of yet another orgasm. She'd lost it, lost it all. He'd gotten what he wanted; what reason for him to come back to her now?

At the entrance of the lot she waited as the light released a burst of rush-hour traffic up Leavenworth; then she eased her foot off the brake. But Runyan came charging across the street, shirtless and barefoot, wearing only his trousers, and she felt a fierce surge of elation. Walking out had been the perfect gambit after all.

Runyan slammed his open hands on the hood as if to stop her, then moved along the flank of the car to her open window like someone gentling a spooked horse. "I thought of a title for your book. *Bad Time.* A con is pulling bad time when—"

She started to laugh, she couldn't help it. Relief, but he couldn't know that. She took her hotel room key from her purse and held it up where he could see it.

"It's a terrific title," she said. "We can talk about it in the morning. Ten o'clock in the coffee shop."

She let the car ease forward so he had to step back or get his bare toes run over. Not knowing why, she blew him a kiss as she shot into the street just ahead of the next barbarian horde released by the stop lights at the corner below.

Runyan stared after her, shifting his bare feet on the cold dirty blacktop; the kiss she'd blown him burned in his mind. She still could be using him, just trying to find out about the diamonds. He glanced down toward the YMCA, three blocks below, then started to trot in that direction, his bare feet pad-padding on the filthy sidewalk.

Everybody said it in the joint: When you first got out, you were so bombarded with stimuli that you'd be overwhelmed if you didn't stay locked away inside yourself. She had already unlocked him, made him vulnerable.

Just don't keep the appointment with her in the morning. Just stay away. Just forget her.

But he was running now, the blood being pounded back into his icy feet. Passing under a raised fire escape, he leaped up and tapped the bottom step with both hands. Kareem Abdul-Jabbar, tapping in a rebound.

He tried to slow to a walk. All the shit in the world might be coming down on him. He needed control. But somehow he was leaping up and whapping the next ladder with both outstretched hands—Kareem stuffing one on the fast break.

"YAHOO!" Runyan yelled. He leaped up and caught the rung of the next ladder, swung backward and forward, let go to land running, whooping, bounding down Leavenworth like an escaped panther joyous in the streets.

Through the glossy philodendron leaves, David Moyers watched Runyan leap down the far sidewalk like the last day of school, barefoot and shirtless besides. Moyers himself had a stocky, underexercised body which looked heavier than it was because of his habitual slouch and because of his heavy head, which contained a mind with nothing slouchy about it.

He tossed a handful of change on the counter. The ageless Chinese man standing in front of the delicate oriental wall mural with a red sign slapped across it, YES, WE HAVE BEERS, bowed deeply and grinned at him.

Moyers walked slightly splay-footed through the chilly spring evening. His car was in the same lot where Louise had left hers. He'd taken her license number and noted it was a Hertz, not because he suspected any connection with Runyan at the time, but because she belonged in that neighborhood like a gold ingot in a butter dish. With that thousand-a-night hooker stride the Supreme Court should have ruled on, the lobby of the Hilton should have been her hunting ground.

He got his bag of new workout stuff from the trunk and

went down toward the Y, memorable as a phone book. His eyes fed data into his quick, obsessed mind without conscious attention as he thought about Runyan and the woman.

Damn her! He'd been willing to be patient; but three hours of fucking Runyan's brains out had given her a definite edge. She was making things move faster then he'd anticipated, and he didn't like the feeling of not quite being in control.

But Runyan, meanwhile, would have pumped a lot of his strength into her up in that hotel room; now he'd be feeling depleted and a little sad, and already disoriented from hitting the street for the first time in eight years. Maybe it was all for the best; maybe now was the perfect time to brace him up about the diamonds again.

Runyan leaped up to slap his chalked hands into the rings, kipped effortlessly into a full pressout, brought stiffened legs up straight in front of him, toes pointed, then swung legs and trunk down and around and into a planche, his rigid body now parallel to the floor. He was still in his slacks, shirtless and barefoot, revolving now into a shoulderstand with his toes pointed straight at the ceiling.

"Ah, Runyan. Drinking the sweet wine of freedom."

Moyers wore a spanking-new red acetate track suit with white piping; on his feet were white Adidas with a red flash. Runyan pushed into a handstand, triceps bunched beneath his smooth hide, rings vibrating slightly with the effort of keeping them in. After a few moments, he lowered into the shoulderstand again. He'd learned how to tune out interruptions in the joint.

"Have you thought about Homelife General's offer?"

Another handstand, the rings vibrating more noticeably now. Sweat was rivuletting the sharply defined cuts between muscles. He was panting.

"The diamonds returned to us, a percentage reward paid, no questions asked . . ."

Runyan returned to his original pressout position, body vertical to the floor, arms tight to the sides, elbows locked.

"Even if you duck me and recover the stones—" Moyers chuckled disbelievingly— "what can you do with them?"

Runyan began the slow agony of a crucifix—moving his arms out to the sides so his body began to lower into the widening gap between the rings. He was panting fiercely now.

Moyers said reasonably, "We've got tabs on every fence big enough to handle them . . ."

Runyan's stiffened arms were straight out from his shoulders with his entire weight supported by his lats, delts, and the bunched, rock-hard trapezius muscles.

"Israel? Holland? As a convicted felon, you can't get a passport . . ."

Runyan lost it, letting go with his left hand, swinging like a chimp, then dropping lightly to the floor.

"The little lady took it out of you, didn't she?" asked Moyers with his nasty little chuckle.

Runyan snapped him under the nose, hard, with an index finger. Moyers sprang back in reflex, tears starting from his eyes. Runyan jerked his towel from the leather horse and slung it around his neck. The slapping feet of a couple of joggers on the mezzanine running track above them echoed through the gym.

"Who is she, Runyan?" Moyers, eyes still watering, gamely got in his way. "I'll just check out her license number anyway."

Runyan spoke for the first time. "Rental."

"She had to show them a driver's license."

Runyan seemed uncertain. "I guess you'll find out anyway." His voice was defeated. "She's writing a book."

"Writing a *book*?"

"Exposing the insurance companies."

Then, for the first time since he had walked away from Q, Runyan started to laugh.

CHAPTER 6

Angelo Tenconi pushed the button. The drapes slid open silently to frame the nighttime city displayed by the wide picture window of his Russian Hill penthouse living room. He'd come far and fast from his boyhood, strong-arming lunch money out of little slant kids and ripping off the poor box at Joe DiMaggio's Church.

From the lighted white finger of Coit Tower in North Beach, past the financial district's soaring TransAmerica spike and cold dark Bank of America monolith, to the glittering tail of headlights the Bay Bridge dragged out from the industrial area south of Market, Angelo Tenconi's grasp was felt. A percentage here, a couple of nonreducible points there—a little bit of a lot of people's action.

He caught reflected movement in the window, turned to see statuesque, blond-braided Melodia pulling lace panties up over the dark pubic triangle he had been savaging just moments before. Ran the city's classiest call-girl operation, but she had started on his money and had never been able to get past the vig to touch the principal.

"Wasn't for me, bitch," he said in his deep aggrieved voice, "you'd be turning two-dollar tricks with some slant up one of them alleys off Grant Ave."

He chuckled softly at the flash of real hatred in her eyes. Smart-ass bitch, with her gallery openings and first nights at the opera. Never did it with customers any more. Never gave head any more. *Wrong.* She gave him whatever he wanted, when he wanted it. He *owned* that bitch, the same way he owned Runyan.

He moved toward the phone. The only difference was that Runyan didn't know it yet.

The skinny rat-faced clerk dropped the receiver so it bounced and jerked on its silver flex, jerked a thumb at it, and went down the hall toward the room with OFFICE over the door. Runyan picked it up.

"Runyan."

A grating unknown voice, its owner probably not as tough as he thought but still plenty tough, said, "Who was the bitch picked you up outside Q today, asshole?"

The guy looking in the condo window. Had to be. He said, "My parole officer."

"Don't get fucking cute with me, Runyan. We been waiting eight years, we don't get our cut, you're fucking dog meat."

Runyan's heart plummeted. That damned Cardwell! He said, "Who's 'we'? You got a mouse in your pocket?"

"I told you not to get cute, asshole. You don't even know which way to look."

He hung up. Runyan put his forearm against the wall as he used to do against the bars of his cell, pressed his forehead against it, thinking. Just a Tenderloin hotshot with a long memory? Or somebody Jamie Cardwell had been in it with?

You don't even know which way to look.

Sure he did. Time to dig Jamie out of his rathole.

. . .

The Veterans Administration Assistance Division was in a big new pile of metal and prestressed concrete on Main near the Rincon Annex. Runyan went through dark-glassed revolving doors behind a regal black woman whose hair was corn-rowed over to one side and hanging down in front of her shoulder. Her beauty brought Louise so sharply into Runyan's mind that a wave of physical desire swept through his body like a chill.

Four minutes after the office opened, Runyan was sitting across from a bureaucrat named Harrold, who had a face like a dill pickle and jockied one of a twin row of desks stitching their way down the big barren room. There was a large red number 4 beside Harrold's name plate.

Runyan used the Okie twang of a lifer he'd worked with in the dry-cleaning plant his first year at Q.

"Me an' Jamie Cardwell, we go 'way back to Nam together. I know he's drawin' partial, so I come to get his address off you."

Taking great pleasure in the fact, Harrold told Runyan frostily that their records were confidential. He would have made a good prison guard, Runyan thought. The kind who'd been such a bastard all the way through that he was all buddy-buddy on your release date, because he didn't want you going out and buying a cheap rifle with a good scope on it once you were free.

Runyan tipped back his chair and stared at a corner of the ceiling. "Tet offensive of 'sixty-eight, it was," he said in a far-away voice. "We was short, hadn't but a week left 'fore we was to be rotated home." He brought down his gaze to the dill-pickle face. "Gut shot."

Harrold's Adam's apple worked, twice. "Gut . . . shot?"

"Cong with one a them AK-forty-sevens the slopes made—you remember them, the kind with them little bitty wire stocks an' the banana clips. Stitched old Jamie right across the gut like a sewing machine." The front legs of his chair hit the floor with a bang, and Runyan was on his feet, leaning over Harrold with a fierce expression on his face. "His guts would of fell right out there on the ground if he hadn't got drug out right quick."

"I . . . I see . . ."

"Like shit you see!" yelled Runyan, veins bulging in his neck. "*I* drug him out!"

James (Jamie) Cardwell lived in the 1700 block of Kirkham Street, had an unlisted number, and worked out of the PG&E Division Offices at 245 Market, reading gas and electric meters.

Louise was staying in a fancy chain hotel two blocks from Fisherman's Wharf. The sprawling unitized four stories of rough-cut wood and tan stucco and red metal trim took up an entire block across Mason from the old Longshoreman's Hall. There was under-the-building parking and a lobby opening off an ornately cobbled, bisecting alley.

Louise was alone at a table for two, drinking coffee and eating sweet rolls and reading the morning *Chronicle*. On her table was a stem vase with a single red rose. Runyan, 15 minutes early, faded back from the doorway without being seen, turned, and collided with a florid-faced man wearing a plaid suit that made him look like an auto seatcover. Pinned to one lapel was a big round button, IT'S A SELLABRATION!

Runyan excused himself and went across the lobby with its clusters of small round tables separated by brass-rail dividers, pinning IT'S A SELLABRATION! to his own lapel. He drummed impatient fingers on the wood parquetry check-in counter until a clerk came.

"Graham, Two-Four-Three, my wife left the key for me."

The harried clerk returned empty-handed. "Looks like she forgot, Mr. Graham . . ."

Runyan pushed blood into his face, turning it crimson. "Just how the hell am I supposed to—"

"I'll get you a duplicate, Mr. Graham." His voice tried to be hurried and soothing at the same time.

Over the bed was an indifferent original of Fisherman's Wharf, the artificially bright colors laid on with a palette knife. Behind it, nothing. In the closet, only clothes with labels from chain stores or boutiques meaningless to Runyan. The suitcase was empty, its sweaters and pantyhose and lingerie in the dresser, the cosmetics case nearly so, its contents on the vanity. A Smith-Corona electric portable and several manila folders were on the table under a hanging fake-Tiffany lamp.

One folder was marked CONVICT BOOK and held newspaper clippings (none about Runyan), notes, and a scratch pad with BAD TIME slashed across it in felt-tip, circled and with several exclamation points behind. Runyan felt momentary pleasure before reason told him she would do the same if it were a con.

In a folder beside the typewriter was a newly typed story titled *Assault on the Citadel*.

Every day we are forced to retreat further into the citadel. The enemy does not advance steadily, so many yards a day. He has to fight harder than that for his territory. Foot by foot. Inch by inch.

Runyan lowered the manuscript. A retired army general, whose only family was a daughter, fighting a losing battle against senility. The citadel was his reason. Louise's father, maybe?

Pops, behind the huge old rolltop in his study, a banty rooster of a man with silky white hair and a kindly, pleasant face which had grown more stern with his years as a circuit judge. The shelves jammed ceiling high with lawbooks, in one corner the rack of hunting rifles shared by him and Runyan. Pops, leaning forward, creaking his swivel chair.

"Remember, boy, you can do things you can't walk away from."

Drunk driving? Assault? Runyan couldn't remember what had occasioned the lecture. Three years later, when Pops died, he'd had to break out of the honor farm to attend the funeral. It was then that the court had given him the option: state prison or service in Vietnam. He'd taken Nam. And done a lot of things since that had only proved the old man right.

With a wave of repugnance, he thrust the story away. Why couldn't they just have a day of discovery together—each other, his freedom—instead of creeping around her room and snooping her belongings, full of suspicion and paranoia?

It only took an act of belief and affirmation on his part. Didn't it?

CHAPTER 7

Louise wore wide-wale cords and a puff-shouldered sweater under her Icelandic wool jacket. Runyan had a heavy Navy wool watch sweater under his windbreaker; but Pier 39 was thronged with tourists woefully underdressed for a San Francisco summer. A little black boy appeared beside their reflections in a shop window, dancing and throwing punches at his image.

"I'm fightin' myself in the mirror!" he exclaimed.

Runyan dropped to his knees, covering up. The kid crowed with delight and bounced a few punches off Runyan's forearms before a long male parental arm whisked him off as an angry parental voice trailed away.

"You're never going anywhere else with me for the whole entire history of the world, you hear me talking, boy?"

They made a circuit of the massive hexagonal games arcade in an absolutely stunning din of voices, laughter, music from the two-story carrousel in the center of the building, electronic bleats and whistles, and the popping of guns from the shooting gallery. Chinese youths in black satin jackets with ornate embroidered dragons on the backs yelled and punched each other over the skeeball games. At MAKE A HOOP, Runyan sank bucket after bucket without a miss.

Louise exclaimed, "Why, you're really *good*!"

"For nothing." Runyan immediately tossed the basketball back to the girl attendant. He added sheepishly, "Lots of free time in the exercise yard."

They started off, but the girl called after them: Runyan could choose anything on the top shelf for free. He picked a huge fluffy teddy bear, four feet long with big soulful glass eyes and a soft black cloth nose.

"You clown! What are you going to do with it?"

"What are *you* going to do with it?" he said, shoving it into her arms like a first grader giving a present. So unexpected was the gesture that Louise grabbed him and held him for a few moments; she didn't want him to see the tears in her eyes.

"Nobody's given me a teddy bear since I was five," she said against his shoulder.

They went down the pier arm-in-arm, Louise feeling as she used to on the first date with a new boy. Suppressed excitement, a sense of adventure, a hint of future wickedness, an almost overwhelming feeling of something strange and shining about to happen. What usually happened was the boys tried to make her, and after a few years she started to let them, and the shiningness had gone away and hadn't come back. Until today.

But then her eyes met those of a slouchy fortyish man standing slightly splay-footed in front of a poster display. She jerked back.

"Runyan! That man . . ."

"What?"

He already was gone. There were a lot of slouchy fortyish men with lustful eyes in this world; no use inviting Runyan to share her paranoid belief that those were the eyes which had ogled her through the philodendrons the afternoon before.

"Nothing." She put the heavy, awkward bear back in Runyan's arms. "You can borrow this until we get back to the car."

It started to go bad at the restaurant, as if the slouchy man's lustful gaze had turned their luck sour. She had chosen a large, impersonal place on the second level, its walls covered with rare photos of old San Francisco—the water chute at the Great Highway, the Cliff House, the Sutro Baths, downtown before and after the '06 quake. The sunken dining area overlooked the pleasure-craft marina, with the Bay Bridge a silver parabola in the background.

They ordered, touched their wine glasses, and drank.

"Did you miss alcohol in prison?"

He shook his head. "I missed you."

"You didn't know me."

"I knew you. In my dreams I knew you." He paused. "In my fantasies."

Runyan drenched everything with ketchup and began eating very quickly, casting quick looks around, his left arm forming a protective circle around his plate. Like a dog with its food bowl, she thought, and had to look away, moved almost to tears by a sort of anguished rage. But he caught her look and straightened up quickly, guiltily, jerking away his protective arm and dropped the ketchup-drenched cheeseburger back on the plate.

"Don't apologize, damn you!" she cried.

They left the pier and walked swiftly, aimlessly, not saying much. In a narrow covered passageway between two of the pastel-colored, low-income housing units in the projects off Bay Street, monuments to the hope-filled redevelopment era of the 'sixties, they passed a dozen black and Chinese kids, ranging from eleven down to about five. They were bouncing a soft, basketball-sized rubber ball against one of the concrete walls.

The ball hit a boy of about seven in the forehead; eyes

squeezed tight shut, he started to cry. Nobody paid attention, so he grabbed the ball and threw it into the face of a five-year-old girl. She sat down abruptly and started shrieking. Louise moved to comfort her; Runyan stopped her.

"Don't humiliate her more than she is!" he said harshly.

Now everyone had stopped to stare. The boy, worried, stooped over her with his hands on his knees.

"You ain't hurt, woman," he said hopefully. She yelled louder. He pointed a finger and jeered, ashamed of his own tears a moment before, "*Crybaby! Crybaby!*"

As she fled, screaming, past them, Runyan thrust the huge soft floppy teddy bear into her arms. It was as big as she, its yellow furry feet dragging the ground between her own. She clasped it automatically, her steps slowing, faltering, stopping. She just stood there, hugging it, staring at them with huge wet-stained eyes; then she whirled and was gone between the buildings with her treasure.

Runyan's unexpected *beau geste* brought tears to Louise's eyes for the second time that day. She said gruffly, "Dammit, Runyan, you gave away my teddy bear."

"You ain't hurt, woman," he said.

They started away, laughing, the bad moments on Pier 39 forgotten—and a tall skinny man on roller skates, wearing a helmet with a tiny rear-view mirror attached, whipped by them backwards with only inches to spare.

Louise yelped with surprise, but Runyan sprang somehow backwards and sideways at the same time, his eyes absolutely wild, every muscle of his body rigid with incipient violence. His skull was momentarily visible beneath the roped muscles. After several moments of total rigidity, his face lost its scraped-bone look, and he slowly came erect.

"I saw two murders in prison," he panted. "I was around the corner from three more. You don't do anything. You don't say anything. You just walk away. Otherwise, a couple of weeks later when you've quit expecting it, somebody rams the sharpened end of a pail handle between your ribs in the shower room and you're just blood on the tiles."

She raised a hand to touch him, comfort him, then let it drop. His voice rose, thickened.

"You ask me what I want? I want OUT. Out from under people like Moyers, following us around." He gestured after the skater, his voice ragged with control. "I wanted this to be *our* day, just me with the most beautiful woman I've ever seen, *and I can't do it*! I'm still in prison, I—"

Louise grabbed him and began physically dragging him toward her hotel.

"All day we've been doing what you want to do," she said. "Now we're going to do what *I* want to do."

Astride Runyan in the dim golden light, Louise felt the pulsating contractions begin yet again. She stiffened, cried out, trapped in ecstasy at the edge of pain. Her orgasm triggered Runyan's: His clenched buttocks reared two feet off the bed and his own spasms began. They remained that way for ten or fifteen seconds, frozen, utterly concentrated, as he emptied himself into her with no movement by either of them. Then gradually his buttocks returned to the bed, and her thighs unclenched from around his hips. Without strength now, she gently folded down upon him.

"I wish every day was this day," she whispered into the hollow of his throat.

"Today is this day."

He could feel himself going limp inside her soft hot cradle. He had never known such utter arousal followed by such utter tenderness. He started to say so, but she spoke first.

"I'm hungry," she said.

"In fact, I can't really remember when I haven't been hungry." She dropped the empty oyster shell on the bed of cracked ice, selected another, slurped, chewed, licked the juice from the corner of her mouth as he watched her in awe. "Better have some before I eat them all."

"You already have." He leaned forward. "Your old man doesn't own a liquor store, does he?"

"He manages the Osco Drug in Rochester, Minnesota. Why?"

"The Marine's dream—the deaf-and-dumb nympho whose old man owns a liquor store—"

"So *that's* how I strike you."

"Rochester, Minnesota," he said musingly. "Don't they have the Mayo Clinic there?"

"Runs the town."

As she spoke, a vivid memory rushed back upon her. She could smell the sharp tang of green apples, feel her T-shirt cling to her bony adolescent back with evaporated sweat, rough bark under her hands, the shock and sting in her feet when she dropped to the ground and darted into the bushes lining the fieldstone drywall at Mayowood. The guard's flashlight bouncing and probing unsuccessfully through the orchard.

"The Mayos had a big estate a couple of miles out of town when I was a kid, we used to ride out there on our bikes and steal apples."

"What happened if you got caught? They'd take out your appendix?"

She laughed and shook her head. "I never got caught."

"Were you scared?"

"Petrified. But it was such a delicious feeling."

"I've never been so scared as this last month, waiting to get out," he said, surprising her; she had thought so much openness was impossible for him. "You get scared of freedom. Every con who's served a few years without getting killed or turning queer has learned how to survive inside. You run a couple of bluffs, you get your Levi's pressed and your shoes shined and wear a fancy belt and buckle. You're a big man. But in the process you let yourself get defined by the place.

When you finally make parole, you start getting scared you won't be able to make it on the outside."

"You want them to have stopped the world while you got off?"

"Or at least slow it down so I can jump back on. But they don't." He squeezed her hand. "You. The way you are. Maybe there were women like you around when I went inside, but I never knew any of them. I don't know how to handle someone like you." His tone changed, tightened; his eyes caught hers and held them. "I wanted it to be simple when I got out. So I could *be* out—not carrying prison around on my back. Nothing coming at me. But *you're* coming at me. You—"

"Runyan, you don't have to—"

"Of course I do. You make me feel . . ." He paused. His voice was intense, slightly hoarse. "You turn me around. I've got to handle that. Moyers is staked out on Beach Street, waiting for me to make my move. I've got to handle that, too. Last night I got a phone call that means I'm going to have to get out of this hotel tonight without being seen. All of a sudden my options are limited. If Moyers finds out I'm going . . ."

"Take my car," she said. Her smile was stunning, full of devilish delight. "I'll take care of Moyers. Moyers will never know what hit him."

CHAPTER 8

Moyers was parked in the first space next to the fire hydrant on Beach just off Mason. The garage entrance was across the street, the exit was centered in his rear-view mirror, and by turning his head he could see down the cobbled alley to the hotel entrance. If they tried to leave, he'd have them nailed.

Slouched behind the wheel of the Datsun, he wondered if they were up in her room right now, doing it again. Almost eidetic images of the woman, nude, in various abandoned positions upon the bed, flashed through his mind: In each of them, Moyers, bare-assed and shlong at the ready, was about to perform upon her whatever sexual act her particular position seemed to encourage.

He forced his mind away, to himself before the parole board, saying the things that had gotten Runyan out of San Quentin. Brilliant.

"I believe he knows where those diamonds are, and I believe he will try to recover them shortly after his release. In doing so, he will violate the terms of his parole. He will be returned to San Quentin, Homelife General will make recovery, and the interests and aims of society will have been served . . ."

Louise Graham opened the off-side door, slid in beside him, and slammed it. She wore a clinging soft grey wool dress which, without displaying anything, suggested everything.

"You have any coffee?" she asked. "It's freezing out and I left my coat up in the room."

Moyers forced himself to look away from her body while he considered the problems her presence suggested. He shot a quick look at the entrance and his rear-view mirror, then reached down for the Thermos, a deliberately sleepy look on his face.

"I hope you left Runyan up in the room too."

She eyed the coffee greedily. "Dead to the world."

He gave a coarse laugh as he unscrewed the top of the Thermos. "Fucked himself to sleep, huh? After all these years without any."

"Oh goody," she said tonelessly. "It knows how to talk dirty. I was so afraid it wouldn't." She held out the plastic cup from the Thermos and he poured steaming coffee into it.

Okay, nothing cheap about her. Brains and sensitivities to match her looks. Which made her more dangerous. Why had she come here? Probably to try and pump him about Runyan. Or about himself; he could be a factor in the equation she hadn't expected. She could be as curious about his role as he was about hers. He switched tacks.

"Runyan tells me that you're a writer."

She nodded. "Louise Graham." She slurped coffee and made a face. "Vile but hot."

"Moose-shit pie—but good!"

She surprised him with a husky laugh that affected him like her languid fingernails running up his spine.

"Don't try so hard to shock me. I started out doing newspaper obits; you ever listen to the jokes undertakers tell between cadavers?"

She started to take another drink of her coffee, bumped her elbow on the door handle, and cascaded hot coffee into her lap.

"Ouch!" she yelled. *"Damn!"*

Moyers snatched out his handkerchief and sopped at the spill, his fingers almost greedy in their movements. Before she pushed his hand away, he had felt the firm twin curves of her inner thighs coming together, had brushed the mound of her pudendum even through the wet wool of her skirt.

"Thanks," she said coldly. "I can manage."

Moyers belatedly looked down the alleyway to the hotel entrance, checked the garage exit in the rear-view mirror. Nothing moving either place. With her coffee spill, Louise had given Runyan just enough time to whip the Lynx out of the garage exit and around the corner, out of sight. Her ruined skirt apparently forgotten, she plucked a box of Winchell's doughnuts from the dashboard.

"Any of these left? I'm starving to death."

Moyers doubted that, having observed them in the hotel dining room, but he wasn't going to argue. He had to get as much as he could from her about Runyan's plans without letting her know what he was doing. It wouldn't be too tough: She was bright enough, but he was a professional.

"So," he said, "you must have come out here for more than my doughnuts."

"Don't bet on it," she said, biting into a sugar glaze. "Newspeople are the world's original freeloaders."

Runyan stopped just beyond the wide concrete apron and, by the light of the streetlamp 30 yards down the alley, looked across the car at the street loading door.

In his mind, a gun went off.

The door was shoved violently open and Runyan, eight years younger, head back and arched as he yelled distantly, fell out through it. Clinging grimly to his attaché case, he struggled to his feet and reeled toward the car, leaving an irregular blood spoor across the concrete.

Stony-faced, Runyan watched himself come shambling up the tunnels of memory and through the closed door of the Lynx, a man made of smoke. He could feel the hairs on his arms rise, as if that younger, crippled, more innocent and wilder self were trying to reintegrate with this stunted prison parolee.

Moyers watched Louise take the final bite of her third doughnut and wash it down with hot coffee. He had a vivid desire to lick away the tiny wetness of powdered sugar at the corner of her mouth.

"I get the feeling," said Louise as she poked around in the box for another doughnut, "that you don't believe a damned thing I've said. So just *pretend* I'm a writer working on a book. Just *pretend* I wrote to Runyan in San Quentin and that he wouldn't even come to the visitors' room to meet me . . ." She looked up. "You like the ones with *hagelschlact* on them?"

"Hagel-what?"

"Those little chocolate bits."

"Oh. No. Go ahead."

Dammit, she *couldn't* be a writer. Any woman who made you want to come just by eating a doughnut had to live by sex. But she couldn't just be a prostitute, either. She was too much herself, she lacked that sophisticated fantasy persona men paid the top-drawer callgirls to possess. So whoever had sent her was a genius. Just-released cons were always after anything hot and hollow with hair around it; but here Runyan had been given the Mona Lisa to cope with.

"In fact," she said, "just pretend I'm a journalist after a story and tell me all about Runyan—who he is, what he did, why he did it, why you're after him. Okay?"

Tomorrow he'd have to run her car plate; meanwhile, she

was dangerous because she made him just ache to tell her things.

"Okay," he said. "Eight years ago, Runyan hit a wholesale diamond merchant for two-point-one-three-million in top-quality uncut stones. He got shot by one of the guards but got away, then crapped out from loss of blood and went off the freeway north of San Rafael three hours later. They got him, but no diamonds."

"If they didn't have the diamonds, how did they prove—"

"Diamond merchant's attaché case in the car. Guard's bullet in Runyan. His blood type on the floor. Positive I.D. by the guard who shot him. From Runyan they got nothing. He stood mute at his trial."

"Where is San Rafael?"

"Marin County. North across the Golden Gate Bridge."

Crossing the bridge, the younger Runyan squinted into the fog at the lights of oncoming traffic. An auto horn trailed angry sound past him, he jerked the wheel over: yellow rubber lane markers flew in every direction as he plowed through them before getting back into his own lane. The bridge's foghorn gave a disconsolate bellow from its nest beneath the roadbed.

In Louise's Lynx, Runyan tried to reconnect with that younger, brasher, colder self again, tried to recapture the rage and pain; but they were emotions in another man's dream. Even the diamonds were an abstraction, something to deal away to Moyers for the reward which then would buy off last night's caller. His life had started today. Louise was reality.

Louise brushed powdered sugar off the clinging fabric in her lap. Moyers could almost feel his own fingers there, beneath the skirt, caressing up her inner thigh, slipping under the elastic legband of her panties to . . .

He said, "I've never bought the image of Runyan the papers

played up at the time—romantic cat-burglar type, in it as much for the kicks as for the money . . ."

"Why not?"

"This job screams for someone inside, and someone else to dispose of the gems afterward. Someone he was going to meet when he went off the road."

"Then he would have had the diamonds with him."

Moyers shook his head. "If he shows up with the stones, already half-dead, they just finish him off and split one less way. But if he shows up half-dead *without* the stones—"

"Of course," said Louise. "They have to keep him alive to tell them where he hid them. But he never made the meeting, and so they never . . ." Abruptly, surprisingly, she shuddered. "So they'd be waiting when he got out. No contact, no threats, no nothing. Just . . . waiting."

"That's why he'll have to come to me eventually," said Moyers complacently. "I'm the only game in town."

She opened her door. "If your reconstruction is right."

"It's right."

She went back across the street, her heels ringing loudly on the pavement. He watched the movement of her backside with carnal lust.

The headlights swept across the ancient, oddly tilted tombstones of the old cemetery. In Runyan's mind, the Bel-Air nosed to a stop, lights and motor still on. His younger self opened the door and fell out on the ground. After a long time, that earlier Runyan dragged himself erect, his hands leaving wet red smears on the door, window, door handle.

Beside the hotel's lobby entrance was a small intimate bar called The Lubbers. Tucked inconspicuously away above it was a dark, cozy private drinking room with only two tables and a view of the street entrance through dark-tinted windows. A bulky bearded man in a red and black Pendleton, calling himself Leo Cronin, finished his drink so Louise would have time to get back to her room. Then he went down to the pay phones in the lobby.

Louise lay on the unmade bed with her forearm over her eyes. She had thought taking on Moyers would be fun; instead, it had brought back all the old despised memories. Smoke, and booze, and uncounted rows of coke. Lights that were never turned off, slots that never stopped clanging, the dealers' smooth tones, the muted click of chips, the babble of the suckers as they poured their case money down the toilet of house odds.

Moyers, in his own narrow little company-man way, was one of them, his cesspool thoughts as easily read as the top line on an eye chart:

J Q X T   WHAT I WANT IS SODOMY
P W K A   GIMME HEAD ALL THE WAY

Men, all men. Except Runyan. She sat up abruptly. God, she wanted him back here with her. *In* her, coming in her, what was she going to do? When he came back, she would tell him. All of it. Every . . .

The phone rang. She snatched it quickly off the hooks, but the heavy familiar voice was not Runyan's.

"Goddammit, where you been? I been ringing for—"

"Out. Busy." Her voice was shriller, brassier, catalyzed into reaction by him. "Don't push, damn you. That was the arrangement. I come in, make contact . . ."

"Well, what about it? He fall for you?"

"How should I—"

"You know, don't try to shit me. You can smell them in rut. That's what you're good at."

Dear God, did she have to tell him? Unwillingly, she said, "He's hooked. Hard." As if she were being ill, vomiting everything out, she added, "He's out in my car right now." Then she plunged despairingly into the gyre of betrayal she had to enter one way or another. "I think he went to get the diamonds."

Climbing in the first predawn light, Runyan could see the little twisted tree on the crest. Bigger twisted tree, now. That night he'd used the tire iron as a sort of crutch, but still had fallen twice before he reached the tree with his sack of diamonds. Half hanging against the trunk, he'd vomited blood, then had gone down the far slope to the massive, oddly shaped boulder on which he'd practiced rock climbing and rappelling techniques. Fell on his knees beside it, started to dig with his tire iron . . .

Runyan, carrying Louise's tire iron, could almost hear the clink of metal against stone. In 20 minutes he'd have the diamonds, he'd take them back and tell Louise all about everything . . .

"Let me tell you," said the bearded Cronin into the phone in the lobby, "I want you out of there tonight."

Louise reeled as if struck in the face. Before she had a chance to tell Runyan . . . what? What could she tell Runyan?

"Are you still in Vegas?" she asked in a dull voice.

"Where the fuck else would I be?" snapped the man in the lobby. "But I have a man in San Francisco to take over."

"Whatever you want."

"I want you out of there." He hung up.

She paced the room, stopped and looked at her face in the mirror. Acid in the face. That's what they had threatened. And he'd wanted her, desperately, and even weak blustery men sometimes found courage in desire. So he'd stood up to them. Or maybe bought them off. Either way, she owed him.

So, betray him, betray Runyan—she was really only betraying herself anyway. She whirled to stare at the love-rumpled bed behind her.

"Damn you, Runyan!" she cried. "You were supposed to be a creep!"

She fell across the bed and burst out crying.

Runyan leaned against the twisted tree and burst out laughing. Bitter laughter, edged with despair. As if in mimicry came one of the intricate broken calls of a mockingbird. A jay raucously challenged it, and a California quail whistled liquidly from a far slope. Dawn was almost here.

Runyan looked down the slope once more at the half-built unit of a not-yet-occupied subdivision. The site was still early-morning deserted, and the boulder was gone, blasted to rubble by a subdivider's plans. Gone with it were Runyan's hopes. The diamonds no longer existed.

CHAPTER 9

Louise was wearing a tam and a Burberry; it was only when the cab went by that her face, framed in that gleaming dark hair, registered with Moyers. He muttered a startled curse and U-turned after the cab up the Embarcadero. Very cool, very clever, going to check into some other hotel, figuring he wouldn't follow her, leaving Runyan to slip out with her car and join her later. Leaving David Moyers in the dust. And she had almost gotten away with it. Would have, if he hadn't been such an old hand at keeping ahead of the opposition.

When this was all over and Moyers had recovered the diamonds, whoever the hell had hired her wouldn't be too happy. She might need someone to take care of her. That might even have been her real purpose in sneaking out to his car last night—laying the groundwork for a new liaison in case she missed with Runyan. Naturally, she would think of Moyers as her next move.

Louise didn't think about Moyers until the cab was up on the skyway heading for the airport. Huddled bleakly in the back seat, staring out at the serrated teeth of the financial district as the early morning light struck their glass caps and steel inlays, she suddenly thought, My God, that creep from the insurance company is going to be following me. She almost turned to look out the rear window, but controlled the urge.

He'd figure she was on her way to check into a new hotel in the belief he wouldn't follow her—so of course he would. When she ditched him, he was going to take it personally and really go after her: So, what did he know, and what could he find out?

He knew her name and the license number of her U-drive. From that he could get to the car rental company, and would have ways of getting into their files—probably just punch her up on the insurance company's computer.

That would give him her Nevada driver's license number, her credit card number, and her Vegas residence address. She caught her own reflection in the driver's rear-view mirror. *They had threatened to throw acid in her face.* Everything dead-ended in Vegas, everything was billed to that address where she hadn't lived for over a year . . .

So, point him at Vegas.

Runyan parked on North Point, around the block from where Moyers would be staked out, and went in a side entrance of the hotel. He didn't have the diamonds, but he couldn't let Moyers know he had gone looking; he would have to think up ways to stall the rough-voiced man who had threatened him on the phone. If they had been there, it all would have been so simple. Now . . .

Now, nobody was going to believe they had been lost in the building of a new subdivision. He could hardly believe it himself. Moyers might be just mean enough and sore enough to get the parole board after him. Violating an ex-con's parole was the easiest thing in the world; any minor infraction was enough to send him back inside.

Walking down the corridor from the elevator, he knew he was going to have to come up with something. Before he had gone inside, it would have been easy; he always had half-a-dozen possible burglaries lined up. But now he was on parole; he almost needed permission to go to the bathroom. No jobs cased and probably no guts to do one anyway.

The only illumination was from around the edges of the drapes. The bathroom was open, its door open. The bed was as they had left it from their love-making.

"Louise?"

Down in the coffee shop. He was halfway back out of the room when he froze. The typewriter and manila folders were no longer on the table.

He hit the lights; the room sprang into bold relief. No cosmetics on the vanity. The closet area was stripped. Suitcase and overnighter gone. He yanked out the empty dresser drawers, dropping each on the floor as irrational panic became rational certainty.

She was gone. Cleared out. No note, nothing. Just gone.

He sat down on the bed as if his legs could not support his weight. There had to be an explanation.

She'd left the car with him . . . With the bill unpaid.

She'd gotten a call, long-distance, her father back in Rochester was sick, sinking fast, there'd been no time for a note to Runyan . . .

There was always time for a note—if you wanted to write one. He stood up wearily. She'd been after the diamonds all along. But if so, why clear out before he recovered the stones? Before there was any chance for her to get them for herself?

What if she'd come to con him out of the diamonds, then had started to feel something for him, as he had for her, and couldn't go through with it? That would explain just disappearing, it would explain the lack of a note or a goodbye . . .

Didn't she know that he didn't care what she'd started out

to do? That yesterday was the first day of their lives? That today was all that counted?

The room yielded nothing to help him find her. But stuffed in the wastebasket were two manila folders. One was the CONVICT BOOK folder, including the sheet with his title BAD TIME slashed across it; the other was ASSAULT ON THE CITADEL. He took them with him; in some way, they confirmed his feeling. She *had* come to scam him, and when self-revulsion set in had discarded the files as too painful to keep.

Somehow he'd find her.

As Moyers pulled up, Louise was walking into the terminal beside the porter carrying her bags. He stopped behind the taxi that had brought her, walked up to the driver's open window and gave the man a swift glimpse of a silver badge he carried for times like this. A replica of the SFPD badge in size and shape, it had long since ceased being even marginally legal to carry.

"Daltinski, Airport Security," he said in a bored voice. His rubber face had become set in the cop mold, his eyes had turned bleak. "That fare you just dropped. Which airline?"

"PSA. She said she was catching a flight to Vegas."

Moyers didn't thank him; cops didn't. He got back in his car and followed the arrows for a return to short-term parking. He couldn't risk leaving his car in front of the terminal—they were very quick to ticket and tow violators here, and he had to get back to the hotel as soon as he knew for sure where she was going. Her catching a plane just didn't fit into any scenario he could devise, and her getting this far away from Runyan just couldn't be made to make sense. Unless . . .

Unless she was just a goddam writer after all. She gets her interview, gets a good fuck from the ex-con—something to tell the monthly writing club about over drinks—and off she goes. But then why leave her car behind?

Easy. She has her Runyan interview on tape, he casually offers to turn her car in for her . . .

But Moyers couldn't be *sure*. And if they *had* run a game on him, and he was out of touch with Runyan, then he damn sure better not get out of touch with the woman.

Toeing her bags forward in the PSA line, Louise kept a wary eye out for Moyers—if he got here too quick she'd have to think of something else. But her luck held. She collected the ticket she had ordered from the hotel, and checked her bags.

"I also need a ticket to Las Vegas on your flight through Burbank," she said to the clerk. "For a Louise Graham. She doesn't have any luggage."

"That flight leaves in eleven minutes," said the mustachioed, uniformed agent as he made out the one-way ticket.

Moyers trotted along the moving beltway, up the two flights of escalators to the main terminal lobby, and shoved his way through the throngs to the PSA flight board behind the ticket counters. The Las Vegas flight was marked DEPARTED. He got the PSA reservations number from a pay phone.

"PSA, Ms. Laurence, may I help you?"

"Yes, my wife is taking your ten a.m. flight to Las Vegas from S.F. International, it just left and I wanted to make sure she caught it. She was cutting it awfully fine. Graham, first initial L."

"Thank you, sir." There was a pause as she tapped into the computer. She came back on. "She was ticketed and had a reservation made just before departure time, Mr. Graham. There hasn't been time for the passenger manifest to be turned in by the personnel on the check-in gate, but the records we do have would indicate she made the flight."

He thanked her and hung up, then used his phone calling card to contact a Las Vegas detective he had used in the past.

"Louise Graham, twenty-nine, blue-green on brown, five-eight in heels, hundred-and-fifteen pounds, wearing a Burberry and a light blue tam. She's arriving on the next flight from SFO through Burbank. Everything you can get on her in a hurry."

"She expecting us?"

Moyers thought for a second. "No. But I'd rather you got made than lose her. I'll call for a preliminary report in . . ." he checked his watch. "Three hours."

"You got it."

Moyers personalized his tone. "Wife and kids?"

"Fat and sassy—in that order."

"They usually are," said Moyers.

As soon as he left the terminal, Louise emerged from the labyrinth of book shelves in the lobby tobacco shop from which she had been watching him. With a touch of irony, she bought Erica Jong's *Fear of Flying* to read during the 45-minute wait for the plane's scheduled departure.

CHAPTER 10

While the soft drink driver was filling the coin machines outside the conference rooms, Runyan stole his uniform cap. He went into the men's room and used his pocket knife to cut off the cloth COCA-COLA badge, then wrote "LOUISE GRAHAM, Wharfside Hotel, Rm 243" on the manila envelope holding the two folders he had taken from her room. Down in the left-hand corner, underlined twice, he added "URGENT."

Carrying the folder and wearing the cap, he shoved his way through the conventioneers and vacationers to the reception desk. He slapped the envelope down in front of the clerk.

"American Messengers. I get no answer from Louise Graham in Room Two-Four-Three. They said to get her forwarding if she had checked out. They'll have to fly this to her right away."

Without a second glance, the clerk went to confer with the cashier, returned with a slip of paper and the address.

"One-Seven-Oh-Two Mojave Road South, Las Vegas. No zip."

Runyan folded the slip and stuck it in his windbreaker pocket. "It'll be hand-delivered anyway. Thanks, pal."

He strolled out of the hotel. The big man known as Cronin came down the stairs from his vantage point above The Lubbers Bar and followed him out. Cronin was well over six feet tall; besides his mackinaw he wore a battered yachting cap, sunglasses, a grey-shot beard, and scuffed thick-soled boots that had gotten a lot of wear but which made him walk as if they hurt his feet a little.

Forty minutes after Runyan had gone, Moyers went past the striped barrier arm and cruised the underground parking garage looking for Louise's car. First alarm and then anger bubbled up as he realized it was no longer there.

Louise, on a plane to Vegas.

Runyan, gone with her car.

Report the car stolen? Wrong play. He didn't want Runyan back inside, he wanted him out here where eventually he would make his run for those diamonds.

Unless he was getting them right now.

No. That didn't make sense. He'd had to hide them at night, in desperation. At night would be the logical time to recover them. And so far, he hadn't had a night out from under Moyer's surveillance.

He showed his I.D. to the same desk clerk on whom Runyan had worked his messenger scam.

"Homelife General Insurance, we carry the personal liability for the hotel." He had no idea if they did or not, but he could be sure the clerk knew even less. "We need the forwarding of a Louise Graham, checked out this morning . . ."

"Sure," said the clerk. "Room Two-Four-Three. One-Seven-Oh-Two Mojave Road South, Las Vegas. A messenger was here half an hour ago with a package for her, I had to—"

"What kind of package?"

"Manila envelope."

"Manuscript size?"

"That would be about right, yes sir."

Could be. A manuscript, galley proofs, research material—the possibilities were endless. He got the address from the clerk, started to turn away, then turned back again.

"Which messenger service, do you remember?"

"Uh . . . American? I think that's what he said."

"What did he look like?"

"You know. Cap. Jacket. Medium height, medium build . . ." He brightened. "Like a messenger."

Moyers headed for the pay phones. Runyan? Could have been, if she's skipped out on him while he was sleeping. But why? Called off? By whom? Someone in Vegas?

He used his credit card to get the Las Vegas number he had called earlier from the airport.

"Stark Investigations."

"Rich—Dave Moyers again, I—"

"I was hoping you'd call, Dave. My man at the airport reported in five minutes ago. Our lady was a no-show. Ticketed and reserved, but not on the plane."

"Goddammit!" exclaimed Moyers. "It stopped in Burbank, could she have—"

"Negative," said Stark crisply. "We've got good contacts at the airport, my man got a look at the passenger manifest."

She'd been standing somewhere in the airport terminal, watching him take the bait. Well, that answered the writer bit. No way.

"I have an address on her," he said. "Seventeen-Oh-Two Mojave Road South."

There was a long pause, then Stark's heavy voice said, "I won't know 'til I see the building, but some of those places out there are connected."

Moyers was silent for a long moment himself. Connected. Two million in eight-year-old hot jewels didn't seem sufficiently heavy action for wise-guy interest as elaborate as this;

but it could be some soldier running his own show, with the organization raking a percentage if he came up with anything. That made sense, and would explain her expertise, her impact. She would be the very best.

"That in itself would mean something," he said. "Get what you can. If it's a dead end, spend some money around town to get a line on her. Stay on her until I tell you to stop."

"Will do."

"And bill this to Homelife direct, not through me. I don't want my name on it if anything heavy is going down."

"Got you," said Stark cheerfully. "Hell, Dave, the company pays a lot quicker than you, anyway."

Finally, Moyers called his office, told them to call him on the mobile phone when they had the Hertz location that had rented the car to Louise. Maybe he could pick up Runyan again when he turned the car in. Failing that, a stakeout on the Westward Ho-tel in hopes that Runyan would show up there before going after the diamonds.

Five minutes before Moyers found out that Louise had rented her car at the Hertz Main Office on Mason Street, Runyan had parked it in one of the return lanes there, had gotten out, and had walked away after dropping the key and paperwork into the slotbox provided for credit-card customers. He had already worked the rental agreement for all its information.

The same Las Vegas address she had left at the hotel. And a Nevada driver's license.

Las Vegas was a long way from Minneapolis where she supposedly had been working on a newspaper.

He walked aimlessly, unaware of the car tail being conducted by the big bearded man in the mackinaw.

The stewardess leaned across the empty seats to ask Louise if she wanted coffee, tea, bouillon, a drink perhaps?

"Oh. Nothing, thank you."

She nodded her warm empty smile and went on. Louise, with a window seat not because she cared but only because the plane was not crowded, watched the endless Western landscape unroll far below her.

She felt drained. Had she done the right thing, just leaving like that? Hadn't she owed Runyan an explanation, right from the beginning? Las Vegas. Getting out with her face still pretty, but owing the man who had gotten her out. Certainly Runyan could have understood that she needed the diamonds, not for herself, but to pay off the debt? Would have been willing to work something out together?

Then she would have been free to take the thing with Runyan wherever it led. Even if it led nowhere in a matter of months, or weeks—even days. Wouldn't that have been better than this . . . this self-loathing?

Stop it. Men weren't that way. There was very little reason to suppose Runyan would have been even the least bit interested in sharing the diamonds he'd given eight years of his life for. He hadn't wanted *her*, he'd wanted her body. He would have refused . . .

Oh hell, he *had* wanted her. She *could* smell it on them, the desire, the wanting. She'd become an expert in that. So, better to have ended it here and now. She'd get over him. She'd gotten over men before, as she'd gotten used to being used by men—and to using them in turn.

She found to her amazement that she was crying silently; or rather, that tears were running down her face without her having any conscious awareness of them. She used kleenex from her purse to wipe her eyes, then resolutely studied the view.

Runyan wouldn't give her up so easily. He'd be looking for her, trying to find her, get her back. Of course he would. There was no way he could do it; but the fiction that he was trying seemed somehow to comfort her.

Runyan got five bucks worth of quarters from the middle-aged change lady in a porn palace a block from Hertz and started working the phone. No listing for Graham, Louise, in Las Vegas. None in Minneapolis, either. Of course she might have a listing in some outlying bedroom community, but he was just hitting the high points here for his own peace of mind.

Okay, one more shot and then admit that she'd just ditched him, pure and simple. He dialed Rochester information and asked for a listing for Osco Drugs.

"Downtown store or Apache Mall, sir?"

"Uh . . . downtown store. But better give me both."

She *hadn't* lied about that, she had been from Rochester—or at least knew it pretty well. Osco Drugs didn't sound like a chain. Apache Mall would have to be a shopping center, probably more recent than the downtown store. *He manages the Osco Drug Store in Rochester, Minnesota . . .*

He dialled the number, fed in quarters.

"Osco Drugs."

"Mr. Graham, please."

"Just a moment, sir."

Graham had a slightly querulous voice with the slight Midwestern twang. This was not the general of Louise's story, trapped in the labyrinth of his own failing mind.

"Do you have a daughter named Louise?" asked Runyan in a heavy official voice.

"Why, yes, we do." Very quickly. "Who is this? What's happened? We haven't—"

"Lieutenant . . . um, Costanzo, San Francisco, California, police. A man who was in an accident had her name in his wallet, giving you as her reference. If you could give us—"

"I find this very unusual," said Graham suspiciously. "In the man's wallet, you say?"

"That's all we know, Mr. Graham. We were hoping you could help us identify—"

"Our letters to Louise have all come back for at least a year from some place in Las Vegas, out in Nevada, and the phone was disconnected a year ago, we had the sheriff's office out there check. A different woman lived there, she'd never heard of Louise." His voice rose, got almost shrill. "What sort of trouble has she gotten herself into now? If she thinks we're going to pick up the pieces for her again she . . ."

Runyan hung up. Not hard to see why Louise had left home. But it did nothing for him; he'd hit a stone wall with her.

He found a bar, had a drink. Stared at himself in the mirror. Fighting the mirror, old-time bartenders used to call it. Time to quit thinking with his cock. Louise was lost to him, gone forever. And he was still in the vise. Moyers. The unknown on the phone—that man wasn't going to give up.

Runyan was going to have to fit himself back into that skin he had sloughed, have to become that earlier, harder man he had been before Q. The man he had come out of prison swearing to himself he would never become again. In the process, he was going to diminish inescapably the man he had sought to become—but he might just stay alive.

He finished his drink and went out to catch a bus. Time to get a handle on Jamie Cardwell, so he could find out what was coming down on him.

CHAPTER 11

The bearded man who called himself Leo Cronin started the car and popped another dexie when Runyan came out of the bar. Had to stay awake and alert until Runyan got somewhere isolated enough to do it. His hand strayed to the cheap plastic suitcase on the seat beside him. Do it, get the diamonds off the body, get away unseen.

Shirt pocket, maybe—Runyan would know that pants pockets could be picked too easily. Or maybe a money belt—which would mean a few extra seconds to get the damn thing off the body, so the set-up had to be right.

He watched Runyan get on the bus.

Two million dollars.

Even fencing the stones in Vegas for only a percentage of their retail worth would get him out of trouble and set him up in style, *really* set him up. Him and Louise. She wouldn't leave if he had the diamonds.

He checked his rear-view and followed the Number 76 bus out Sutter, still thinking of Louise. If she ever found out he'd aced Runyan, he'd lose her. But she was on her way back home by now, believing he was still in Vegas. He'd tell her his man in San Francisco hadn't been able to get the stones, but it didn't matter because he'd won *big* in Vegas, *really* big, enough to get even and a hell of a lot more besides.

Guys like Runyan always seemed to get whatever they wanted, but not this time. Runyan had Louise for the moment, but . . .

Goddamn, he'd almost missed Runyan getting off the bus. He had to drive right by him, pull up across Van Ness, and hold him in the rear-view mirror. Not easy, with a man you knew you were going to kill. Six, seven years ago he'd maimed that nigger in Detroit with a fucking knee-drop, but he'd never killed anyone before.

Fucking Runyan he was going to kill.

A bus came and went; Runyan stayed where he was.

Could he do it up close this way, in daylight, looking him right in the eye when he pulled the trigger? Things could come up in you at a time like that, could mess your head around for that vital moment. And he could be so worried about getting away afterwards that he could screw it up, too. Better just hope . . .

Runyan got on another bus. Everything was okay when he was moving, didn't have to think. Think of the two million. Two million dollars in diamonds, all his, fair and square, finders-keepers . . .

Runyan got off the 71 Bus at 23rd and Kirkham. From the pay phone at a drugstore in a small neighborhood business area, he called Jamie Cardwell's unlisted number. He let it ring 12 times, then hung up. On the way out, he bought a clipboard and a pad of cheap lined paper which he clipped on top of Louise's manila envelope.

The Sunset District south of Golden Gate Park was working-class: stucco and frame row houses built in the 'thirties. Until then, the whole area had been empty shifting sand dunes. Even now, often, the fog didn't burn away until noon and was back by four. But today it was bright and beautiful. A good day for Runyan to check out the terrain, find his edge.

Cardwell's house was in the 1700 block, sharing side walls with the adjacent houses and with the usual under-the-house garage. Curtains shut off the front windows. Runyan went up the terrazzo steps to the inset front door and held his finger on the bell for a long time. No response.

As he started down, a small dark vivacious woman in her forties, with piercing brown eyes and an old-fashioned kerchief tied around her head, came down the sidewalk wheeling a cart full of laundry. "You looking for Miz Cardwell, she's a nurse over to the Shriner's Hospital on Nineteenth and Moraga, they don't like personal visitors on the job?"

"It was Mr. Cardwell I was—"

"Five o'clock." He realized she was foreman of the local information factory, punching the neighborhood time clock. "He gets off work to PGandE at four, picks up their little girl Patty from the playground and comes straight home. If there's anything I can help you with?"

"That'd be the playground at . . ."

"Sunset at Twenty-ninth, between Lawton and Moraga."

"Thank you *very* much," said Runyan, starting away.

She called quickly after him, "I could tell him you were asking for him, Mister?"

"Harrold. From the Veterans Administration."

Staring after him, she exclaimed aloud, "His disability pension!" Her face cleared and she triumphantly trundled her cart down Kirkham.

This might be the place, Cronin thought with quickening pulse. Over on the far side of the block-wide park were slides and a monkey gym, but Runyan was sitting here alone in a swing. Cronin actually had opened the plastic suitcase before he paused. The broken-down 12-gauge shotgun inside had eight inches hacksawed off the barrel so it would fit.

Not good. Not smart. Sure, Runyan was alone, but across the street were houses. Inside would be housewives sitting on their butts while their husbands were out working to support them. And sure as hell one of them, during a commercial in her soap opera, would wander over to gawk out one of those windows—and see him blowing the back of Runyan's head off. No thanks.

With mingled regret and relief he shut the cheap plastic suitcase again. He had to be patient, wait for dark. In a city in daylight, he wasn't going to find enough isolation to do it.

But what if Runyan was here to meet his fence? Okay, then he'd show the guy a sample of the merchandise, then set up another meet—negotiations in something like this took time . . .

Tonight, after dark, while Runyan still had the stones on him. Then he'd take them to Vegas, fence them through his connections there. He had a lot of connections in Vegas.

Patty was about eight, wearing a blouse and a jumper short enough to show bony knees too big for her legs. Her eyes were a waif's eyes, shy and downturned. Reddish hair worn long, lots of freckles. She would be a beauty some day, but right now, Runyan thought, she was just the skinny little daughter of a busy mother trying to make the best of a lousy marriage.

She set her blue book bag precisely at the foot of one of the sloping metal poles supporting the swing apparatus. As he'd known she would, Patty chose the swing furthest from his.

"I used to swing a lot when I was your age," he said.

She shot a quick sideways look at him, wild as a fox kit.

"I know," said Runyan, "your mommy told you not to talk to strangers. That's what I'd tell my little girl if I had one."

Abruptly, she said, "My daddy."

"I'm a friend of your daddy's. His name is Jamie."

She looked over at him openly now, forgetting to swing. "Nobody but Mommy calls him Jamie."

"I knew your daddy a long time ago, Patty—before you were born. Did he ever tell you about being in the war?"

"That's why his stomach hurts so he has to take a lot of drinks and yell and throw things. To make the hurt go away."

"I *bet* he has to take a lot of drinks," said Runyan. He stood up. "Would you like me to push you while we wait for your daddy? That way you won't have to pump."

When Jamie Cardwell got out of his lousy old Datsun, he could hear his daughter's delighted shrieks from the swing just out of sight up the grassy slope. Patty was the only really great thing that had happened to him in this lousy world. He'd be long gone from here without her. But shit, Betty'd get her if there was a divorce, what with his lousy credit and his record as a drinker. What'd they expect of a guy got as many lousy breaks as he did, for Chrissake?

Cardwell started up the slope, panting immediately from the effort. He had changed from the solid chunky Cardwell of Runyan's nightmare. His cheeks were slack, leathery now, his face ruddy with the habitual drinker's high color. Self-pity calipered his mouth; his eyes were set in sockets of discontent. A whiskey-drinker's paunch hung over his belt.

Dammit, a man had to drink to kill the memories the gook bullets had stitched into his gut all those years ago.

Lousy breaks.

He lengthened his stride. Some bastard was pushing Patty in the swing.

"*Hang on tight!*" the guy yelled, and ran through underneath her, releasing the swing at the very far end of its arc, so she was hung out parallel to the ground for a delicious microsecond, clinging to the ropes for dear life and shrieking with the excitement of her own daring.

"What the hell do you think you're doing?" Cardwell yelled at the guy. He stopped Patty on the backswing, jerked her off the seat, held her against his aching stomach. "Honey are you okay? How many times have I told you about strangers in—"

"Strangers, Jamie? I'm hurt."

The voice froze him. He felt the blood draining from his legs. He wanted to fold his arms across his slug-stitched gut and fall down on the ground in the fetal position and just stay there.

Runyan was back on his own swing, grinning at Cardwell. Cardwell darted looks from him to the girl and back again. She had her face in her hands, trying to hide her tears.

"Why . . . why don't you go play on the slide with the other kids, Patty?" he said in an uncertain voice, as if asking Runyan's permission with the question.

Patty darted away without a backward glance.

"I had a chat with your V.A. caseworker, Jamie." There was nothing in Runyan's face at all. Not hatred, not pity. It was as if he were having a discussion with a picket fence. He idly drifted himself to and fro with little stabs of a toe in the dust. "I told him about saving your life in Vietnam, and he told me where to find you." The voice got soft and terrible. "You *do* remember me saving your life in Vietnam, don't you, Jamie?"

A great feeling of self-pity washed over Cardwell. "I wish you'd of left me to die! I never—"

"—never get any breaks," said Runyan. "I know, Jamie. Like eight years ago, when you owed some Shylock money and came to me with this setup where you worked. Pleaded with me . . ." His voice was so low it was almost a whisper. "Seven years in Q, hoping it was just you and me in on it. But it wasn't just you and me, was it? I had a phone call the night I got out of Q, Jamie."

"A . . . phone call?"

Runyan's eyes burned Cardwell with their coldness. "Which one suggested blowing me away and splitting it up between the rest of you?"

Cardwell wanted to lie. He was *going* to lie. But he couldn't. Not to those eyes.

"They ... didn't know until ... afterwards ..." His heart was pounding so hard he thought it was going to fly to pieces. He burst out, "I *had* to, Runyan! There wasn't enough, not with what I owed the Shylock, and the other guy's cut, and what I needed to ..." He swung his arm toward the children screaming their delight across the park. "*She* was on the way ..."

Runyan stood up with a bitter laugh.

"I thought when I came out of Q that I wasn't going to have to go into the shit again. Shows you how stupid a man can be, doesn't it?" He looked off across the playground. "Eight years in the can." He looked at Cardwell. "How old is she, Jamie? Eight? Nice kid. I'll be in touch."

Cardwell watched him walk away, tears of anger and frustration in his eyes. Yeah, he'd be in touch, and Cardwell would get shoved around again, would have his little Patty threatened again. He didn't have any other options. In this lousy world he never had any options, never got any breaks. But he knew one thing: He needed a drink, bad. Right now.

CHAPTER 12

Cronin shifted the cheap plastic suitcase between his feet and leaned back further into the shadows, feeling equal terror and elation. Catty-corner across the intersection was the Chinese restaurant; in a few minutes Runyan would walk the half block from there to his hotel and would go up to his room.

And would be killed.

It had to be tonight, because Runyan *had* met the fence in that little park just as Cronin had suspected. He'd been too far away to hear anything, but after sending the little girl away they'd obviously argued price.

With a shotgun, you couldn't miss, right? BING BANG BOOM, it was done. The guys in Vegas sometimes joked about it—making their bones, like that; now he was going to do it. What the hell, Runyan had killed guys in Vietnam, hero, decorated, all that shit. Now it was his turn. That's just the way life was.

73

. . .

Moyers adjusted his rear-view mirror slightly when it picked up a heavy bearded guy angling across the street to the Westward Ho-tel, checking in with his cheap plastic suitcase. Transient neighborhood of meaningless guys like Runyan who'd screwed up their lives and would never get on track again.

Except that Runyan had slept with Louise Graham. A loser like Runyan didn't deserve that sort of luck. Since his divorce a few years before, Moyers hadn't had much luck with women he hadn't paid for, and Runyan and Louise together had really burned him. So he was glad that now Runyan would be carrying her in his mind, wondering where she'd gone and why, wondering what he'd done wrong—and not able to do a damn thing about it except hurt.

Runyan was thinking of Louise and hurting. He wished he had the resources, knew the angles to find her again. But what if she hadn't left because she was ashamed? What if she'd merely been called back to report to whoever had hired her in the first place? Stew about that one for a while, Runyan.

The bright-eyed black-haired old Chinese man brought his check and laid it on the table.

"Good soup?" he asked. Runyan had eaten fried chicken.

Runyan rubbed his stomach and grinned. "Very good soup."

The old man giggled and went away with Runyan's money.

Cronin came out of the room he had rented and tapped the sawed-off muzzle of his shotgun against the bare low-watt bulb of the nearest hallway ceiling fixture. The bulb shattered with a subdued POP which drifted down thin warm shards of pale glass.

He moved down the hall on silent stockinged feet, repeating with the other lights. Nobody came from any of the rooms at the sound of the bulbs breaking. Most of them were pensioners, what did they have to do anyway except go to bed early and stare at the ceiling in the dark?

The cross-hall was now very dim. Runyan would have just enough illumination to see the keyhole of his door. Which was the last thing he would ever see.

Runyan turned into the darkened cross-hall, checked at the slight crunch of glass under his shoe, then went on. For those few moments, still distracted by Louise, he rejoined the majority of mankind. Because most men, their survival no longer dependent on identifying another by his scent, the rate or timbre of his breathing, the precise click of tendons in knee or elbow, have lost the ability to perceive physical threats instinctively.

But Runyan was a born survivor. He had been around the corner from three murders in prison because his survival instinct had stopped him from turning those corners. Those same senses now strove to warn of danger, but Runyan was ignoring them.

Even when he stepped on the second litter of fragments, he didn't connect it with himself. Since nobody knew the diamonds no longer existed, nobody could move on him, right? He was safe.

By the dim light of the window, he bent to thrust his room key into the lock. Twenty feet down the hall, in darkness his eyes could not penetrate, a fingertip slid surreptitiously across a shotgun safety catch.

Runyan heard the tiny metallic click of his father's shotgun safety before he heard the beat of the pheasant's wings as it rose from the clump of red rye grass, and he knew, I'm between him and the light, and was already throwing himself backwards and sideways out of the closed fire-escape window while his conscious mind was still trying to fit the key into the lock. The frame and curtain six inches above his hurtling body splintered and shredded with the shotgun roar.

Runyan hit the slatted metal platform in a sideways tumble

and kept rolling, right over the edge. Grabbing handholds recklessly, he dropped down the steel framework of the fire escape like a monkey, careless of torn palms, ripped clothes, or gashed skin, jinking first one way and then another to create a difficult target. Tricks that had become second nature from years of rock climbing and rappelling in the Sierra carried him down.

He hit the alley on the balls of his feet with his knees flexed, tucking and rolling even as he landed, tight up against the side of the building. Two more shots ripped down at him, the goose pellets whining and rattling down through the metal struts of the fire escape to gouge the blacktop where he had landed a second before. None hit him.

He heard the *squeerk!* of metal two stories above even as running footsteps pounded down the alley from the street. Runyan rolled quickly back from the wall and sprang to his feet, so when the cop's torch beam impaled him he was standing in the middle of the alley, gawking upward.

"Shots!" he cried, turning toward the light, shielding his eyes with one hand, still pointing upward with the other, *"Up there!"*

The uniformed beat cop swung his light up, service revolver in hand. The fire escape was empty except for tattered remnants of curtain blowing through the gaping second-floor window.

"Second floor!" yelled Runyan.

The cop ran for the mouth of the alley which would take him around to the front of the building, gun still in hand.

Cronin ran lightly down the hall, rage at Runyan's escape turned to fear. Just as he had rehearsed it in his mind, except now, goddammit, he didn't have the diamonds. He didn't have anything. Jesus, lucky it was the sort of hotel it was—nobody even stuck a head out of a room. He threw the shotgun into the suitcase, shoved his feet into his boots, and ran down the hallway toward the front stairs with his laces flapping.

He was at the head of the stairs when the street door opened and the cop came pounding up. He ducked, terrified, around the edge of the stairwell, and the cop ran right by toward the back of the hotel without even a turn of the head.

He went down the stairs very quietly and quickly, keeping to the edges so they wouldn't creak. It was just over two minutes since he had fired his first shot.

Moyers, standing outside his car and wondering what had happened, saw the big bearded guy come back out, still carrying his suitcase, and go up the hill with his boot laces flapping. Drug pusher, rousted by what had sounded like gunshots, getting out while he could? But if they had been shots, why had the cop let him go? And where was Runyan, who had entered the hotel less than five minutes before?

Runyan slouched to the mouth of the alley, hands in pockets, just another nighttime Tenderloin drifter. He checked and faded back into the shadows without any quick movements.

Uphill across the street was Moyers, standing beside his parked car, staring intently at the entrance of the hotel. Staked out, probably had been there when Runyan had come carelessly home. *Damn* prison, the way it had dulled his reactions! Would he ever be what he had been, thinking with his gut, survival instincts in control, instead of being distracted by his emotions to the point where they nearly got him killed?

Survival thinking meant getting a wall at his back and keeping a clear field of fire in front of him.

He was loose right now. Nobody had a finger on him. Not Moyers, not whoever had tried to kill him, not whoever had called him, not Cardwell, not anybody. Not even Louise.

He had to make his own moves, follow his own rules, use his own logic. No more counterpunching. From now on the initiative had to be his. Otherwise he was going to be dead.

And in that hallway a few minutes ago, his body had told him what his mind, in his misery, had perhaps forgotten: that he wanted desperately to be alive.

CHAPTER 13

At 5:30 a.m. the bearded man, no longer bearded and no longer Leo Cronin, went bust at the $100-minimum blackjack table at the Arabian Nights Hotel on the Vegas Strip. Angel Morgan, security manager for the casino, was looking down idly from the security catwalk above the mirrored ceiling when the player took a hit and went bust with an eight.

Angel chuckled. "Hey, Manny, you see who I see?"

Manny Arnheim, the casino manager, was dressed in Western clothes and hand-tooled boots, but looked like Hoagy Carmichael—a limp cigarette even dangled from one corner of his mouth.

"Jesus Christ," he said in a grating voice, "the fucking clown is back!"

"And bust," said Angel.

"This surprises you? The man's a degenerate."

"Should I call down the street? I hear he's into them for a pretty good bundle."

"Naw," said Manny, losing interest, "comp him at the front desk if he needs it. The guy did us a good turn last year, taking that broad out of here, what was her—"

"Louise."

"Yeah. Louise. He got her out of here before we had to do something about her . . ." He shook his head almost sadly. "Good broad, then she gets fucked around in her head and starts wanting to talk to people . . ."

The big man who was no longer Leo Cronin entered the 11th-floor suite, crossed the wall-to-wall, and opened the sliding-glass door to the balcony. Cool morning desert air came in. He stared at distant purple mountains.

Christ, he'd planned to be here with his pocket full of diamonds and his troubles behind him.

Instead, he had fled San Francisco in a panic, sure that if he looked back he would see red lights flashing. Then the stupid trick downstairs, going bust at blackjack an hour after he hit town. So here he was, riding one of Manny's comps at the front desk because he was over the limit on his plastic.

They always said a shotgun was a sure thing, shut your fucking eyes and cut down a roomful of people. But he'd missed. *Missed!* With a fucking shotgun! Fucking Runyan had moved like a snake. He'd never seen anybody move so fast.

So now what? He had to think. Maybe there was still a way. Runyan knew somebody had tried, but he didn't know who. Louise had said there were others after the stones, and Runyan had been moving around, showing himself, talking with the fence . . . Hell, for sure he'd think it was one of the others.

So, keep all his options open. Call the airlines, call his office, call Louise. And call room service for some breakfast and a Bloody Mary or two. Maybe he could salvage it after all.

Louise was asleep when the phone started to ring. She knocked it on the floor where the receiver kept making squawking tones. When she found it and brought it up to her face, they became words: " . . . hell are you doing? I've been ringing this goddamn thing for—"

"I *was* sleeping." She used her brassy voice.

"Sleeping? It's six in the morning."

She sat up under the covers, hugging her drawn-up knees. Her old-fashioned flannel nightgown, shapeless but practical, went with the big brass-steaded bed and the colonial-looking patchwork quilt.

"You called me up to tell me that?"

"I called to say I'll see you this afternoon."

"Why didn't you wait until this afternoon to spoil my day?"

"Goddammit, Louise, do you always have to be that way?"

" 'To be what we are, and to become what we are capable of becoming, is the only end of life,' " she said. "How about that? Stevenson at six a.m." She realized she was still a little woozy. Two Restorils, two Valiums, and a hot milk with rum and honey in it, just to get to sleep last night. "I suppose I should ask you how your man made out with the diamonds in San Francisco, but you know what? I'm tired of talking with you."

She hung up the phone.

It started to ring again as she got out of bed and walked across the rag rug to the typing table in front of the window. It was the sort of room one's grandparents grew up in, hard-wood dresser with an oval mirror, family portraits on the walls in cherrywood frames, slow-ticking brass-pendulumed grandfather clock as tall as she was. The bird in the gilded cage. Maybe work would keep her from getting depressed over his return.

She sat down and turned on the typewriter. The phone kept on ringing. She kept on ignoring it.

The fat woman's lower jaw moved up and down like a puppet's in its motionless bib of fat.

"There is a gas leak. I can smell a gas leak."

"Lady, there isn't any gas leak. I checked."

"I tell you, my gas bills have never been this high."

Jamie almost told her where to put her gas bills, but instead just walked away, leaving her flapping and squawking like a hen with its head cut off. Let her complain. They couldn't fire him—he was on disability and PG&E was a public utility.

Hell, he'd forgotten to read her meter. Well, it was all that goddamn Runyan's fault anyway, showing up yesterday and threatening his kid. He pull that shit again, Cardwell thought, swinging up into his brown and tan PG&E truck, he'd shoot the fucker again, and do it right this time.

Runyan was sitting against the far door, his hands empty but great bodily harm in his eyes. All thoughts of killing him skittered desperately from Cardwell's mind. Runyan made it worse by saying, "Somebody tried to blow me away last night, Jamie. Was it you?"

"I . . . I got loaded last night, Runyan. You can ask Betty if you don't—"

Runyan sighed and looked out the windshield. "One of the others, then."

"I didn't tell them you were around." He grabbed at Runyan's arm. "You've got to believe—"

His head was rammed right down inside the ring of the steering wheel, so suddenly he didn't even know it had happened. Runyan's voice came from somewhere above and behind him.

"You tried to kill me once, Cardwell. Don't ever lay your fucking hands on me again."

He was abruptly released. The strength in those hands had been terrifying. He pulled himself erect. His jaw ached where it had been slammed against the steering post. He risked a look over. Runyan was different from yesterday. Harder. Colder. Cold as the grave.

"Are they morons, or what?" he asked. "Is one of them stupid enough to think I'm carrying the diamonds around with me?"

"Look, Runyan, leave me out of it, okay?" Cardwell whined. "I got a wife and kid to support—"

"Your wife works and your little girl goes to public school," said Runyan coldly. "You draw disability from the V.A. and you have a steady job at union scale and seniority. Give me the names of the others, *then* you're out of it. Unless they're expecting me when I drop around—then you're back in."

Watching him walk away with the names he had wanted, Cardwell felt a great weariness. It wasn't ever going to end. It was just going to keep on, until he was dead. He'd never got any breaks. They were all bastards, every one of them, and he'd never gotten even one little break at all, never in his lifetime.

Moyers put a ten-dollar bill into the rat-faced clerk's paw, and the rat scuttled back into its hole. The shooting last night had to have been an attempt on Runyan, but nobody had seen anything, nobody was hurt or dead, and the cops weren't going to waste much time on it. Runyan's stuff was still in his room. Moyers would have to hold the stakeout to see if Runyan would chance coming back for it.

He went to the phone, picked up the receiver, was about to drop his two dimes when he thought: the drug pusher. The big bearded guy in work clothes. His suitcase had carried a broken-down shotgun, not drugs: instant, not progressive death. In and out, blip, blip, blip—very professional.

Except that he'd missed. Which said that Runyan was very damned good indeed. Well, Moyers had seen him work out on the rings. He moved like quicksilver in the palm of your hand.

A professional hit. But by whom? Louise's Vegas connection? That seemed most likely.

None of that got him any closer to Runyan. But this might. He put in his dimes and tapped out his number. When a secretary answered, Moyers said, "Mr. Benjamin Sharples, please."

. . .

Runyan was nursing a cup of coffee in a cafe next door to a sex devices store which also rented gay video porn movies. His two hundred from the parole board was almost gone; there was enough to pay a week on the room he'd rented by phone, sight unseen, on Bush just beyond Franklin, but not much more. He had to get his stuff out of the Westward Hotel, and he had to dó it without Moyers catching on. He couldn't have Moyers looking over his shoulder any more, because somebody else might be looking over Moyers's. After last night, staying loose meant survival.

Three young white male whores in chains and black leather came in and took a table near his. They looked him over, mistaking the nature of his interest. The blond one came to Runyan's table and sat down.

"Hello, darling," he said.

Behind the eyeshadow and rouge he was not over 16, wearing a cup to make his scrotum look sexually engorged. Runyan had seen dozens of them at Q; most of them, handed around the cellblock like a box of candy, were reduced to rubble in a week. Those who survived came out vicious and usually deranged. This one hadn't started the downward spiral yet.

Runyan tore a twenty-dollar bill in two and dropped half of it on the table along with his room key.

"Westward Ho-tel, around the corner and up the street. Second floor rear by the fire escape. Clean it out, clothes, a chess set—everything except the yellow gym bag. Leave that."

"What is this, a joke?" demanded the kid in a half-scared, half-angry voice. This wasn't as simple as opening some John's zipper in the men's room.

"Easy money," said Runyan. "Somebody's waiting outside the building—knows me, but doesn't know you."

"If this is a setup, my friends will hurt you. Bad."

Runyan didn't speak, so after a moment the kid took the

maimed twenty and the key and stood up. As he started to turn away, Runyan said softly, "Your friends?" The kid paused. Runyan said, "*They*'re the hostages."

The boy stared at him through mascaraed lashes, then walked out with a single scared backward glance. While waiting for his return, Runyan looked up the South of Market Loan Company in the phone book.

CHAPTER 14

When Runyan entered the storefront office on Mission off Fifth, around the corner from the old Mint, a little bell screwed to the top of the door tinkled. A secretary with grey-streaked hair and a long nose was pounding an antique electric typewriter as if it were the chest of an unfaithful lover. Runyan's clothes and chess set were under his arm in the supermarket bag the hooker had brought back to him.

The secretary stopped typing, her mouth slightly open so he could see an inverted V of rabbit teeth behind her upper lip.

"He's expecting me," said Runyan.

She pointed over her shoulder with a pencil she jerked from her hair, jammed it back, and assaulted her paramour again as Runyan crossed to the door.

The inner room was a windowless box with an old-fashioned bottled-water stand against the back wall next to an equally old-fashioned coat rack. Nothing old-fashioned about the steel-set-in-concrete under-the-floor safe; not even oxy-acetylene would touch that baby.

A fleshy red-headed man with his shirt sleeves rolled up almost to his shoulders was sitting behind a desk with a brass plaque on it: PATRICK DELARTY. He had freckled muscular arms with fine red-gold hairs glinting on them. A cigar jutted from the center of his mouth as if he'd seen too many old newsreels of Franklin Roosevelt. Red brows which he pulled down over hard blue eyes in a frown made him look like a clown with only half his makeup on.

"Something?"

Runyan's eyes roved across the room to the other, empty, desk. Its plaque read ANGELO TENCONI. Angelo Tenconi was one of the names given him that morning by Cardwell.

"Tenconi."

"Workin' North Beach today," said Delarty.

Out on Mission Street, Runyan checked his watch. He'd made another appointment with his parole officer to report his change of residence. By the book. That way, nobody could claim he'd violated his parole and send him back inside.

Benjamin Sharples was a bland-faced mid-thirties, with a stubborn chin and mean eyes and the habitually irritated expression of a Persian cat. He was reading in a stamp dealer's catalog about a pair of 1893 Columbia Expositions, unused. Seven-hundred catalog, a thousand retail. Not the sort of thing you find in the post-office booklets on the memorial first day covers currently available, but he wanted them. Very badly.

His secretary opened the door and stuck her head in. On the outside of the glass was:

STATE DEPARTMENT OF CORRECTIONS
REGIONAL PAROLE SECTION
BENJAMIN SHARPLES

"Mr. Runyan," she said.

Sharples felt a tightening in his stomach. He nodded, quickly shoving the stamp catalog under some folders on his desk. He was studying one of them at random when Runyan came into the room. After a full 60 seconds, Sharples clapped shut the folder and looked up snappily.

"Runyan—is that it?"

"Same as three days ago," said Runyan. "I have a new residence address. Sixteen-Twenty Bush Street."

"Why have you moved from the . . . um . . ." Sharples was finally consulting Runyan's file. "The Westward Ho-tel?"

"They've received a demolition notice. The building is going to be torn down."

Sharples closed the file. Runyan continued to stand there. Sharples looked up with irritation which seemed laced with nerves. "Was there anything else?"

"I'm waiting for you to write it in the file."

Sharples flung the file open almost petulantly and wrote the new address on the COMMENTS sheet with a ballpoint pen. He turned the file around so Runyan could see the address and the date written there.

"That satisfy you?"

Runyan turned and left the office without speaking.

Sharples blew out a long pent breath, then wrote the address again, this time on a sheet of scratch paper which he folded into his morning newspaper. He picked up a porkpie hat with a red feather in it off one of his filing cabinets, put the hat on his head and the newspaper under his arm, and walked out.

Sharples maneuvered his white-bread tuna and his coffee, white, through the noontime office workers to one of the standup counters at the rear of the little sandwich shop on Mission and 18th. A slouchy mid-forties man, finishing a cup of coffee while reading his newspaper, grudgingly made room for him.

Sharples laid down his newspaper to arrange his sandwich and coffee fussily. The slouchy man put his newspaper down beside it to wipe his mouth with a napkin from one of the shiny metal dispensers, picked up Sharples's folded newspaper while leaving his own, and walked out. He had sleepy eyes and an unmemorable face and a slightly toed-out walk.

Sharples removed from the newspaper the sealed white envelope containing his bribe money for Runyan's new address. He put the envelope unopened into his inner suitcoat pocket and started eating his sandwich while reading the newspaper. Maybe this would be enough for *one* of the 1893 Columbia Expositions.

Runyan's room on Bush Street was almost half again what the Westward Ho-tel had cost, but it was neat and clean and sunny, with real lace at the windows and a nice framed Audubon print on the wall. He sat on the edge of the bed and, with the Phillips-head screwdriver on his Swiss Army knife, loosened the two tiny screws holding shut the shallow secret compartment of his handmade chess board.

Inside he had hidden the nearly $800 he had saved during his seven years in San Quentin. Since any money a prisoner is trying to remove unofficially from any California State penal institution is considered contraband, no matter how honestly accumulated, Runyan had chosen this method of bringing out his meager hoard. Others used the backing of photos or paintings, the bindings of books, the heels of their shoes.

Perhaps Runyan should have tried one of those more common methods. The compartment was empty. His money was gone. By flashing his ace around to show he had only one day left, he had given whichever con had ferreted out his secret enough time to grab Runyan's stash.

Big Art Elliott had planned to be back to his office by three, but it was closer to four-thirty when he walked in. Gladyce was typing a letter he'd given her last week, handwritten on lined yellow paper. His mind seemed to go blank when he tried to organize his thoughts aloud, and besides, the blond secretary didn't take shorthand anyway. She had the job because her husband Hank was a long-haul driver in the union.

"Any calls or anything?"

She jerked a thumb at his private office. "Or anything," she said darkly. "The auditors were here waiting when I got back from lunch."

He remembered then. He made a disgusted but resigned face.

"They give you any idea of how long they'll—"

The phone rang and Gladyce held up a hand for him to wait.

"Amalgamated Truckers Local Number Eight-Seven-Three."

Art stared moodily at her as she covered the receiver with her hand. "A man calling long distance, says he's your brother?"

"Oh yeah, sure." Art grabbed the receiver and talked standing beside her desk. "Where the hell are you, kid? I thought you were coming up after you got . . ." He paused, shooting a glance at Gladyce. "After, you know . . ."

"Something came up, I'm still in San Francisco," said Runyan's voice. There was an embarrassed pause. "I hate to ask, Art, but is that offer of a loan still good?"

"Hell yes, whadda ya need? Five-hundred? A thousand?" Art winked at Gladyce as he listened. Gladyce had a nice jiggly chest and wore blouses that showed plenty of it. Maybe he'd take a crack at her one of these days when her old man was out of town on a run. "You got it. Give me your address, one of the guys in the local down there will drop it by in an hour."

Runyan gave him the Bush Street address, which he wrote on Gladyce's scratchpad. Runyan thanked him and promised to get the money back as quickly as he could.

"Whenever—or never," laughed Art. "Remember, I'm expecting you up here in a few days." He hung up and gave Gladyce the slip of paper. "Give Tandis a call down in San Francisco, tell him to have somebody drop five hundred from petty cash around there this afternoon. My kid brother'll be waiting. Tell him I'll send him a check to cover it this afternoon."

"Sure, Art." Gladyce leaned forward, a wistful look on her face and her best attributes offered for inspection. Art inspected. Nice. Damn nice. "I wish somebody would give me five hundred bucks just like that," she said.

"Maybe we ought to talk about it sometime," said Art.

"Hank's not coming until tomorrow night."

"Well, maybe I'll come tonight," he said, straight-faced.

"Count on it," said Gladyce.

Going into his office, Art realized that Gladyce looked a little like his ex-, Dolly. Even had that look in her eyes like she was gonna pop the weasel any second when she was talking about money. Fucking broads, they were all the same.

Angelo Tenconi turned in at a tiny Italian deli a few doors down the street from a large supermarket on Columbus Ave. He was just about finished with his rounds. He had collectors and, if necessary, muscle to make collections in the rest of the city, but North Beach was home base for him. Keep in touch with his roots. Local boy makes good—or I'll break your freaking arm.

Inside, he swaggered through the rich Italian smells of garlic and tomato paste and onion and salami and peppers and basil and olive oil and dried anchovy. Behind the little sandwich counter the old Mustache Pete and his broad-beamed wife, both in their sixties, were chattering volubly in a patois of English and Genovese as they covered the cut meats left over from the noon sandwich trade.

The old man looked up as Tenconi loomed up beside the

counter, starting, in a heavy accent, "Can I helpa . . ." then stopping and going on in a different tone, "Oh. You. Tenconi."

Tenconi thrust by them without speaking and punched NO SALE on the old-fashioned ornate scrolled cash register. As he did, another customer entered the front of the shop. Tenconi paid no attention; in North Beach, he did what he wanted.

He took out the thin sheaf of bills held with a rubber band and counted them. He looked up scowling when he had finished.

"There's only the vig here. Nothing on principal."

The wife burst out despairingly, *"E che vuoi. Sempre l'interesse, sempre piu interesse . . ."*

Tenconi shrugged in cold indifference, meanwhile fighting hidden laughter. Actually, he didn't want these old jerk-offs ever getting to their nut. They'd pay him interest forever.

"Hey, Mama, that's your problem. The supermarket, they got lower prices, good fresh produce, Italian run, they get the business, *capisce*?" He added coldly, "Nobody asked you to borrow money to keep this dump going."

He went out of the store shoving the money in his pocket, savoring the moment as he did every week. He'd worked as a delivery boy for these old *sciagurati*, they'd ordered him around plenty then. Now it was his turn. Jerk-offs.

When he was gone, the other customer appeared from the other aisle. He seemed not to notice their humiliation; instead, he gestured after Tenconi. "Wasn't that Angie Tenconi?"

"Da big man," muttered the old Italian.

"Where's he living these days?" the man asked idly.

They knew, of course. Despite everything, North Beach was still an Italian community where people knew each other's business. Runyan had counted on that.

CHAPTER 15

L ouise, dressed in sloppy, comfortable country clothes that went with the Norman Rockwell room, worked through the manuscript with her ballpoint pen, scribbling revisions, crossing out words, writing a whole new sequence into the right margin. The phone rang. She swivelled to reach down and pick it up.

"Yes?"

"I'm back. We have to talk."

"I thought maybe your plane had crashed." She wrote in another phrase. "*Hoped* it had crashed."

The heavy voice began, "There was a time when you were plenty goddamned grateful to—"

"That was before you started asking me to fuck other men on your behalf," she said. She put down the manuscript page and, with the phone clipped between shoulder and jaw, fed a fresh sheet into the typewriter.

"Why not, you had plenty of practice in Vegas."

"And you wonder why there's nothing between us any more," she said, and hung up.

She forced her mind back to *Assault on the Citadel*. She had written it over again since San Francisco, she thought it was a lot better than the version she had left behind. Writing as therapy? She started to type with the quasi-despairing concentration of impending interruption, dreading whatever scene was to come, but grateful for these few hours.

She wondered what Runyan might be doing.

Runyan walked briskly along the posh Pacific Heights street. Carefully nurtured hardwoods gave the block a slightly Eastern air, as if some early gold-rusher had been nostalgic for Connecticut. He was dressed in black tight-fitting clothes; his shoes were tight-fitting also, rubber-soled rock-climbing shoes that scraped no leather echoes from the sidewalk.

Gatian Sheridan had an impressive Queen Anne Victorian with a steeply slanting driveway which ran up to level off alongside the house and then continue back to the garage where the stable and carriage house once had been. No lights showed, but in the rounded turretlike structure at one corner of the house—a feature of Queen Anne architecture—a window was open.

That would do. If he still had his nerve.

He hyperventilated, went up the slope in a rush, cleared the low picket fence around the planting beds in a nimble leap, landed coiled in the bushes directly in front of the house, and sprang upward—all in one burst of movement. There was the adrenaline constriction in the chest, the feeling that he had to move, do something, act, or he would explode. God, he hadn't known that feeling for eight years!

At arms' length below the decorative trim under the front windows, he worked quickly over to the slot between bays. He chinned himself, kicked one leg up and hooked a heel, levered himself up, and was standing erect on the two-inch-wide trim.

He began chimneying himself up the slot exactly as he had done dozens of times rock climbing before San Quentin, his back against the side of one bay, his feet against the side of the other. His technique was rusty; but from the countless hours of gymnastics in prison he was stronger than he had ever been.

At the top he paused, wedged between bays. Directly above his head was the heavy metal rain gutter. He shook it with one hand, testing it for support; then he swung at arms' length below it, kipped neatly up into a pressout, swung a leg up, and rolled over into the trough between the roof coping and the rain gutter.

The lower sill of the open third-story window in the curving face of the tower was only about two feet above his outstretched hands. As he crouched to spring, a heavy sedan turned into the slanting driveway.

Gatian Sheridan had gone to work in his father's wholesale jewelry business after college at the age of 22. He had convinced old Hiram that if they ever wanted that nice standard 300 percent markup, they would have to enter the retail trade. His father had died a year after Runyan's conviction.

As the lights of his conservative black Mercedes four-door swept across the front of the beautifully maintained Victorian, he noted with a little thrill of anticipation that the tower window was shut.

"I did close it, Norman," he said. "You were right."

The man beside him, who was about ten years younger and quite beautiful, said softly, "I'll have to chastise you for doubting me, Gatty."

A delicious shudder ran through Gatian as he killed the engine and the lights and got out, a soft pale man of 36, exquisitely dressed in a grey three-piece suit with a slight hint of salmon stripe running through it. Norman was taller, lithe as a dancer, with long blond hair that Gatian loved to kiss.

This was going to be some night. First Leontyne Price in *Tosca* and in magnificent voice; now . . . the tower room.

Inside, they went directly up to their adjoining bedrooms to get ready. Norman had spent a year in Morocco learning things that made Gatian weak to think about. He pulled on black silk pajamas, put on his superb velvet quilted smoking jacket, and padded barefoot to the connecting door.

"I'm going up, Norman," he called through it. "I have the new *Tosca* as a surprise for you."

"I can hardly wait," said Norman in those soft tones that raised the hairs on the back of Gatian's neck.

He opened the door with the mirror on it, flicked on the lights, and went up the circular staircase to the tower. The walls were covered with pornographic photos of copulating males; there was another full-length mirror on the ceiling above the king-size waterbed with the mauve velvet spread. He crossed to the expensive unitized stereo and put on the *Tosca*.

The haunting voice of Tosca pleading with Scarpia for her lover's life filled the room. Still crouched in front of the stereo, he opened a small compartment and removed a small golden platter. He did not see the door of the antique armoire behind him open cautiously. From the same compartment he removed a small plastic bag of coke, which he ripped open to heap on the platter, a one-edged razor blade, and a tiny golden spoon.

Something round and metallic and hollow was pressed against the back of his neck. A hand grabbed an agonizing fistful of his hair and jerked his head back. A voice grated in his ear.

"Scream, I'd love it."

Gatian had already opened his mouth to do so. He had never known such mingled terror, revulsion, and excitement in his life. His heart felt as if it was going to stop, but he also had an instant and rock-hard erection.

The man pulled him to his feet and walked him across the

room to the ornate, mirror-topped coffee table. "Put the tray on the table," he said, "then sit in the chair."

Gatian did so, hoping the robber wouldn't notice his erection. Or maybe he wanted him to. He didn't know. He was terrified, not thinking straight.

"You . . . you can have the coke, any cash . . ."

The pressure of gun against the back of his neck went away. The man, lithe as Norman but more muscular, with an absolutely marvelous build set off by his tight black clothing, walked around the coffee table and sat down on the arm of the couch. Gatian realized the hollow socket of the candlestick he was holding in one hand was the "gun" that had been pressed against the nape of his neck. He looked involuntarily at the stairwell.

"I wouldn't," said the man. He made no threatening motion of any sort, but his tone jerked Gatian's eyes back to him, and shocked recognition brought another terrified *frisson*.

"Runyan!" he exclaimed. "You're Runyan!"

"Eight years ago, you fingered a robbery of your father's wholesale diamond firm. Pretty neat idea. You collect on the insurance, then peddle the stones later at retail. The one trouble was that I ended up in the slammer for seven years."

Gatian's mouth was suddenly very dry. "I . . . I had nothing to do with . . . any of that, Runyan. I wouldn't—"

"It looks like the insurance set you up pretty well, but your kind always wants more." He leaned forward. "Did you want it bad enough to come after me with a shotgun last night?"

Gatian looked into his eyes and was totally still, suspending even his breathing. Runyan answered his own question contemptuously.

"Not you. You'd come in your pants the first time you touched a gun." He paused speculatively. "Your little friend?"

"Norm . . ." It came out as a squeak. He tried again. "Norman wouldn't . . ."

"Of course not. You wouldn't put yourself in his hands that

97

way." Runyan started around the coffee table, then paused. "Stay clear until I get the insurance man off my back, or there won't be any diamonds. Just . . ."

He tossed the heavy candlestick high in the air, so he was already jerking open the window as it crashed back down through the mirror top of the coffee table, puffing Gatian's coke into oblivion.

" . . . Just seven years bad luck. For someone." He threw a leg over the sill. "I've already had mine."

Norman came bursting up the stairs in black leather bikini briefs and soft black boots halfway up his thighs. He wore a domino mask. He stopped dead at sight of the chaos.

"What happ—"

"Oh shut up!" exclaimed Gatian in a high hysterical voice. He was down on his hands and knees, trying to salvage his coke. At that moment the duet on the stereo ended.

CHAPTER 16

Before Runyan had been sent up, Whitey's had served the best ribs in town. It still did. He dropped the last bone into the rubble on his plate and wiped his fingers with a paper napkin. Whitey's didn't run to steaming finger towels.

The chubby black waitress had pudgy thighs which made *whish-whish-whish* sounds under her black nylon skirt when she moved. Runyan laid a twenty-dollar bill on the counter beside his plate. He was the only white man in the place, which was on Fillmore not far off Ellis Street.

"I heard Sister Sally's man hangs around here," he said. The girl's eyes got old. He chuckled and flicked the bill with his finger. "I'm not heat and I'm not trouble."

After a long moment, she picked up his check and the bill off the counter. As she did, her finger pointed briefly toward the rear of the restaurant. "Flashy Dude," she said.

Runyan looked at the mirror behind the counter; the silvering had come off, giving the black young brash-looking man's reflected image a cloudy Maxfield Parrish effect. He was playing one of the electronic games in the back of Whitey's, all purple and fox grey and ruffles, as if hoping someone would mistake him for Prince.

Runyan sauntered back to stand very close behind Flashy Dude. He said, "Sister Sally." The black man became aware of him by stylized degrees, as if coming up from anaesthetic.

"Go fuck yo momma," said Flashy Dude without turning.

Runyan put a friendly hand on his shoulder and smiled. It was the same smile he had given Jamie Cardwell in the park. His vise-like fingers tightened. Flashy Dude winced.

"Which freeways you want them to find you under, Dude?" he asked in his soft prison-dead voice.

Flashy Dude's eyes went moist, not so much with pain as with the knowledge that Runyan might only be bluffing, but that he didn't have the seeds to find out.

Sister Sally's was on the second floor of a frame house in a totally black neighborhood on Sutter just off Broderick. A block away were the lights and traffic of Divisadero. Runyan went up the terrazzo stairs to the front door of the lower apartment, which was illuminated by a 40-watt ceiling fixture, the bottom of the globe brown and mottled with the bodies of dead moths. The stairway was littered with yellow throwaway shopping newspapers.

The door opened on a chain; music and laughter brought out the smell of smoke and liquor and perfume with them. An impassive eye peered out. The white of the eye was yellow-tinged.

"Sister Sally," said Runyan. "From the Dude."

The door was opened wide enough for Runyan to enter but not so wide that he could avoid brushing against the bouncer as he passed. Quick fingers checked for weapons, went away.

The living room was dimly lit for a spurious seductive look. In chairs and couches lining the walls were half a dozen white and black women in various combinations of revealing underwear, negligees, camis, teddys, and chemises. All were reasonably young, all were attractive, one was beautiful. None, Runyan was sure, was cheap.

Milling around in the center of the room were several black men with drinks in their hands. Their conversation dipped as Runyan went toward the bar which was set up beside the kitchen doorway, but Chaka Khan from the stereo was loud enough to shatter glass.

Behind the bar was an immense black woman with a round jolly smiling face and achingly white teeth and warm brown eyes that bespoke knowledge of and forgiveness for all sins. She wore a billowing *futa* of a thin silklike print material, and moved with a great natural dignity that owed nothing at all to age or beauty.

She was mixing a drink with a rhythmic dexterity that was almost music. In the rich mellifluous voice of a gospel singer, she asked, "What's your pleasure?"

"Taps Turner with a twist," said Runyan.

She gave a bawdy chuckle and shook her head in wonderment. "Mmmm-mmm, that Dude! Whut I'm gonna do with that child?" She raised her voice. "Ambrose, the gen'man's just leaving." As the bald-headed bouncer appeared at Runyan's elbow, she added, twinkling, "You the wrong color in the wrong part of town at the wrong time of night, boy. You ain't careful, Taps be playin' at your funeral."

Ambrose took Runyan's arm in an ungentle grip that made him go numb from shoulder to elbow. He said, "I'm Runyan."

Ambrose hesitated. Sister Sally kept wiping at the same spot with long, circular motions with her bar rag, her eyes fixed on Runyan's face. Then she gave him a huge delighted grin.

"Mr. Runyan," she said, "let me offer my condolences on the loss of your loved one."

Dirgelike organ music rolled tastefully down the hallway of the mortuary from one of the chapellike viewing rooms. The carpet had a thick maroon pile, the drapes were discreetly heavy plush to absorb sound and cigarette smoke. Runyan paused beside the open doorway beside a tasteful plaque, SERVICE IN PROGRESS.

He went through the doorway. A tape-activated organ, unattended, played in one corner of the room. The otherwise empty room was full of pews. At the far end an open casket on rollers was banked with fresh flowers that made him want to sneeze. Lighted candles flickered in ornate brass holders.

The dead black man in the casket did not seem to mind the solitude. As Runyan moved up the aisle he could hear, over the funereal strains, the murmur of voices and could see brighter light coming through the gap between the floor and the foot of the drapes behind the dais. He pulled aside one of the drapes.

Overhead lights bright enough for autopsies made moving puddles of heavy shadow on the blanket that had been thrown over the old-fashioned marble dissecting table. The dice were still with Runyan. He was the only white player among a dozen men. His point was eight. He had an impressive pile of money in front of him.

"Eighter from Decatur," he said ritually.

One of the other players dropped a bill in front of him. "Says twenny," he exclaimed.

"You're faded," said another. "Mother can't keep doin' it all night."

Runyan rolled. The dice bounced against the stop at the far end of the table, landed with two fours showing. The banker raked the dice back to him.

"All right!" exclaimed Runyan, reaching for his winnings.

The thick black hand of Beef, the bouncer, was there before him. Beef had a face to which all possible damage already had been done: seamed and scarred and flattened and bent, with a shapeless nose trying to sniff out trouble beside his cauliflowered left ear.

Beef's other hand took the dice and tossed them to the

middle-aged banker, who had an unlit cigar in one corner of his mouth and a Giants baseball cap on his balding head. He squinted at them against the light, meanwhile running his fingers delicately along the edges for loads, shaves, roughs, or slicks. He nodded and bounced them up and down in a seamed brown palm.

"Uh huh," he said, "suction bevel miss-outs. Damn good, too." He looked over at Runyan. "Musta got them from Lay Dead Dawson up to Q, ain't nobody else does 'em that good these days."

He jerked his head at Beef, and Beef yanked Runyan away from the table into darkness. The banker collected Runyan's winnings with his rake.

Taps Turner sat on the corner of the desk in his office, one ankle-booted foot swinging idly as he counted the stacks of money on the desk. There was a lot of it. He was perhaps 33, dressed in a very conservative $500 midnight blue three-piece suit, a pale blue-on-blue shirt of vertical stripes, and a watered silk tie which caught the light with subtly shifting shades of maroon.

"Damn good night," he murmured over the distant music.

"Best in almost a month," admitted Grace.

He gazed appreciatively at her as she worked the electronic tape calculator with lightning speed. Her hair was natural and very short and her deep brown skin glowed with health. She wore ivory linen slacks and a puff-sleeved sweater that matched Taps's tie in color and had cost as much as his suit.

The door slammed open so Runyan could run headfirst into the wall across the room. He landed in a heap and stayed there, making vague choking sounds in his throat and moving his arms and legs aimlessly. Beef filled the doorway from edge to edge and from floor to header.

"Playin' with shaved dice," he said. His lips had once been split by something blunt and hard, and had been glued back together slightly awry, so he spoke with a sort of rumbling lisp. "You want I should make sure he—"

"I'll handle this mother myself," said Taps.

This jerked Grace's head up; she stared speculatively at Runyan as he rolled over onto his back and groaned. Beef looked from Grace to Taps to Runyan, then sighed and backed out of the room. Taps stood up, hands on his hips, grinning. Runyan crawled slowly to his feet. Grace came out from behind her desk.

"You're some fun guy to look up," said Runyan.

Taps gestured at the stacks of bills, still grinning.

"Got a lot of people would like to drop in 'long about countin' time. I figured you could find me if you really tried."

"That makes you Runyan," said Grace. She didn't offer to shake hands. "You wouldn't be here if you weren't calling in Taps's marker."

Runyan nodded. "I need to score. Big."

"Yeah!" Taps suddenly laughed and slapped his knee. "I always knew you'd come around eventually. The setup is the same—hot bearer bonds in a penthouse safe in Los Angeles . . ."

"How big?" asked Grace with unconcealed hostility.

"One-half of thirty percent of whatever two-point-one-three million in uncut stones, retail eight years ago, would be worth today."

Grace's eyes didn't even flicker, nor did she turn back to her calculator. "If they're under a carat-twenty-five, you have to figure two-hundred-twenty percent appreciation, minimum. So that means you're talking . . . um . . . a hundred-twenty-five dollars shy of seven-hundred-nineteen thousand dollars."

"Bright for twenty-three, ain't she?" demanded Taps proudly.

Runyan was still meeting the hostility in Grace's eyes. He said to Taps, "This setup good for that much?"

"Different numbers each month, but it's the biggest hot

bond drop west of Chicago." He shrugged. "Sure. It'll go two, three times that easy."

"You tap everything over the basic nut I got to crack."

"You're crazy, Taps!" Grace exclaimed. "You and Brother Blood worked it out that he stays in L.A. and you stay up here. It's workin' just fine. You try this, that man's gonna eat you two alive!"

"I don't plan to leave any tracks," said Runyan. "You come up with duplicate bonds good enough so he won't make 'em before he unloads 'em and—"

"You that good?" demanded Grace disbelievingly.

Runyan was still meeting her eyes. "I'm that good."

Taps was leaning back against the edge of the desk, his arms folded on his chest.

"It's gotta wait 'till I can get the serial numbers off the next shipment from my man in L.A. . . . Where can I reach you?"

Runyan walked around Grace's desk to look at the number tape on the phone. "I'll reach you," he said.

"Right enough. Anything you need?"

Runyan took several hundreds off the desk and slipped them into his pocket. "To replace what your gorilla took off me out there," he explained. "And a set of lock picks. I don't have time to make my own."

Taps nodded and Grace opened a drawer in the desk and took out a three-by-five black leather folder with a snap fastener. *MAJESTIC PIX-QUIK* MODEL B was stamped on the leather in gold letters.

"I gets 'em from a outfit in Jersey," said Taps. "They think I'm in law enforcement." His booming laugh was surprisingly sonorous for such a slim man.

CHAPTER 17

Doctor Don was smart-assing his way into his morning-commute stint after the six a.m. newsbreak of KFRC when Runyan got off the 31 Express on Bush and Franklin. Moyers slid a little lower in his car seat as he watched the bus rumble away and Runyan trudge up the hill.

Doctor Don said, "Dave 'The Duke' Sholin is so cheap that his seersucker suit *sucks*!" Runyan looked too exhausted to spot Moyers if the insurance investigator did a tapdance on the hood of the car. Doctor Don added, "Dave Sholin is so cheap that he has a sign on his toilet, 'When the lid won't close, flush it!' "

Moyers switched off the radio and flicked on his micromini-cassette recorder as Runyan turned in at the rooming house.

"Six-oh-eight a.m., Wednesday, the eighth," he dictated. "Surveillance of subject recommen . . ."

He stopped dictating and slid all the way down in his seat. Louise Graham was just driving by in a white current-model Toyota Tercel four-door. He raised his head quickly above the level of window, caught her license as she put on her blinker for the left turn into one-way Franklin Street, and wrote the number in his notebook.

"Surveillance of subject recommences at his new residence address of Sixteen-Twenty Bush Street," he dictated. He did not mention Louise Graham in his report.

Runyan put on the night chain and crossed to the bed without bothering to turn on the light even though the shades were down and his room was quite dark. He lay down on his back on top of the spread, fully clothed, his shoes still on, bouncing up and down a little just because the bed *would* bounce, unlike his cot at San Quentin.

He felt like he could sleep for a week, after identifying the competition and with his visit to Gatian serving notice on them. And now they were setting up the job Taps had talked about incessantly during their years in Q. He had sure never intended to pull another robbery, but what could he do? He was on parole. He couldn't run and they knew it, so he needed cash to buy them off. Damn Cardwell! Why hadn't he worked alone—or at least told Runyan there were others involved?

He'd also have to figure out a way to get Moyers off his back, but staying alive had first priority. Right now, he was free. There was no way Moyers or anyone else could have a tag on him that he could think of, which meant the initiative had passed to him for the time being.

He set the alarm for four that afternoon and went to sleep with his lock picks under his pillow. He'd need them tonight.

It had been a lousy day for Angelo Tenconi. One of his debtors had got himself all stirred up and had balked at making payment, so Tenconi'd had to have the fucker's leg broke. Thing is, how was the freaking guy going to keep up his payments, he's in the hospital with a broken leg? But it had to be done; an example had to be made.

Then there was this thing with freaking Runyan, coming around to Gatian and, for Chrissake, *threatening* him. Two million freaking dollars, and Runyan running around like some kind of nut case.

He was almost glad when he let himself into his penthouse and found the remains of last night's party still littering the living room. He dropped his topcoat on the floor as he punched out a three-digit number on the phone.

"Tenconi, penthouse. Get a fuckin' maid up here to clean up the mess."

"Yes, sir. Right away, sir."

He hung up feeling gratified. He owned the building, so he didn't have to take shit from anybody. He went around the wetbar on which the phone stood, jerking down his tie as he did. From the fridge he got an ice-cold beer, jerked the tab and dropped it on the floor as he recrossed the room toward the hallway. In passing he flicked on the TV and threw the remote on the couch.

Runyan came through the hallway arch and delivered a truly stunning kick to Tenconi's balls. Beer sprayed and the can went flying. Tenconi, knees clamped together, dropped slowly to the floor making the sound bath water makes leaving the tub.

Runyan jerked Tenconi's .41 Magnum out of its shoulder holster and stepped back as Tenconi tried to focus on him through pain-blurred eyes.

"Did that get your attention—*asshole*?"

Tenconi began crawling toward the couch like a half-crushed beetle. "You're . . . dead, Runyan . . ." he panted. "Abso . . . lutely . . . fuckin' . . . dead . . ."

On the TV, John Ritter had lost his trousers on syndication and was running around the *Three's Company* set in his boxer shorts while the studio audience howled. Runyan was ejecting the live rounds from the Magnum, plink, plink, plink, onto the wood parquetry at the edge of the rug. Tenconi was now on his side on the couch, knees drawn up, face pasty.

"Next time, you better not miss," Runyan told him.

Runyan snapped the revolver shut and dropped it on the floor, where it made a dent in the varnished surface. He crossed to the door and jerked it open to leave.

A mahogany-faced Chicana maid was standing outside the door with her cart behind her, just ready to shove a passkey into the door lock. Runyan bowed.

"You'd better come back tomorrow. Mr. Tenconi is all balled up at the moment."

He went by her toward the elevator. The maid shrugged to herself and closed the door again. She didn't like being alone in the apartment with Tenconi anyway. He always put his hands on her when she had to pass close to him.

Runyan came out of the YMCA with his hair slicked back and damp from his shower. He'd done a full routine—rings, high bar, parallel bars, the horse. He felt pleasantly tired and hungry as a bear. The face-off with Tenconi hadn't hurt, either. He was getting his edge back.

As he passed between the old ornate pillars flanking the entrance, Moyers fell into step with him.

"You didn't leave any forwarding at the Westward Ho-tel."

"Somebody thought I had the diamonds in my pocket and tried to take them away." In the first space beyond the white passenger zone in mid-block, a car's lights went on and the engine turned over, caught. Deadpan, Runyan added, "You don't carry a shotgun around in your trunk, do you?"

"They're going to get you, Runyan."

"At the trial, the prosecution said I was working alone. Found the combination on the back of the desk drawer—"

"You wrote that there yourself, Runyan. It's an old safe-cracker's trick." He added urgently, "They've had eight years to figure out how to do you in *and* get the diamonds."

"Unless I turn the stones over to you. Yeah, sure."

They were almost even with the car whose engine had started up. The driver honked once, a single short tap. It was a white Toyota Tercel with a woman behind the wheel. The woman was Louise. Runyan's face flushed hot as if he were ashamed of something he had done. *Louise!* What . . .

"Homelife General can offer you the reward for turning in the stones, plus protection from whoever—"

"Old home week," said Runyan, glad of the darkness that hid the almost feverish flush on his cheeks.

He cut across the sidewalk to the car and opened the driver's door. Louise quickly slid over into the other bucket as Runyan started to get in. Moyers belatedly ran across the sidewalk, but Runyan already had the car moving. He looked in the side mirror; Moyers was standing in the white zone staring after them with an unreadable expression. Runyan gave a short snort of laughter, then turned to look at Louise as if seeing her for the first time.

"You didn't know where else to find me, so you waited around until I showed up for a workout. You just couldn't stay away—"

Louise kept her eyes straight ahead. "I missed you."

"But back there in Minneapolis you'd left a hot story on a back burner and you were afraid it would boil over, so—"

"Dinner? My treat?" she said abruptly. "I have to talk with you. Seriously."

"Okay. I used to know a good place over in Tiburon." He stopped by the Golden Gate Theatre as the light fired a burst of pedestrians across in front of them. He had forgotten the excitement of downtown crowds at night. He looked over at Louise. She was much more exciting. He said, "Anybody going to lose any sleep over you if we're late home?"

The green beauty of her eyes was almost painful, like an unexpected blow to a nerve center. She shook her head and smiled. "You?"

The light changed. Runyan made the left into Taylor, edging around because now the pedestrians were flowing that way. He chuckled.

"Well . . . maybe a guy named Tenconi . . ."

. . .

Tenconi had Runyan backed up against the wall with one hand around the back of Runyan's head, the other buried in Runyan's throat. He grasped the Adam's apple; he was going to rip it out and make the freaker eat it. Runyan was making a harsh buzzing noise.

The door buzzer, long and insistent, finally brought Tenconi awake. He couldn't remember his dream, except that Runyan had been in it and that it had been pretty damn good. He checked the luminous face of his watch. Nine-thirty, a little past. He must have fallen asleep on the freaking couch.

The doorbell sounded again.

Tenconi gingerly swung his legs around and sat up. He rubbed his eyes with the heels of his hands. The burning in his groin had subsided, though his balls were still tender to the touch. He fumbled around, switched on the table lamp and squinted against the illumination. The bell rang again.

"Yeah, coming!" he yelled.

Freaking maid, why didn't she use her key? He padded to the door on stockinged feet and put his head close to the panel.

"Yeah? Who?"

There was no response. Tenconi grunted and slapped aside the fancy wrought iron peephole cover and stooped slightly to put his eye to the little glassed orifice. The silenced .38 pressed against the outside of the peephole said PHHHT! and Tenconi spun away from the peephole with only one eye. He was dead before his knees started to buckle.

CHAPTER 18

The Dock Restaurant overlooked the Tiburon marina; from their window table they could watch the yachts rock at their moorings as the red and green jetty lights drew slow colored circles in the air. Angel Island, a dark unlit mass to the left, helped frame the city twinkling across the bay.

Louise set down her wine glass and leaned forward slightly. Her eyes glowed in the light of their candle.

"Now, young lady," she said in mock-judicial severity, "if you would just tell the court in your own words about your abrupt disappearance and equally abrupt reappearance from—"

"Las Vegas," said Runyan.

"Oh," she said, much of her gaiety slipping away. "The auto rental form?"

"And a few phone calls. Vegas . . . Minneapolis . . . Rochester . . ." To her dismayed look, he nodded, "They aren't going to bail you out of whatever trouble you've gotten yourself into this time, but please send money."

"It wasn't always that way," she said, a little bitterly.

"How about stealing apples off the Mayo brothers' estate?"

"Oh, *that* was true. But the book . . ." She waggled a palm-down hand. She finished the wine in her glass; her tone changed abruptly. "You know, when I was in high school and junior college I really did want to be a writer. I wrote all the time—"

"The stories in your hotel room," said Runyan. "Window dressing from a long time ago?"

Louise nodded. "In a way. But it's funny, now I've started writing again. As if wanting grew out of pretending."

"Sort of like you and me, isn't it?"

He kept being able to do that: catch her unawares, surprise her with an insight he shouldn't have been capable of having. Why couldn't it just be as simple as that?

"Exactly like you and me," she said, hating the lie in the remark even as she made it. Runyan nodded again.

"Only your folks hadn't heard from you in a year, and you weren't listed in Minneapolis, and none of the Las Vegas data was any good any more. So . . ."

She held out her glass, glad of the respite, fighting the oddest compulsion to break out crying. But at the same time realizing that he was different from when she had walked away a few days ago. Subtly in command now, more sure of himself, more aggressive. Was it her coming back to him, showing her vulnerability, or was it something that had happened while she had been gone?

Runyan finished the bottle into both their glasses. "So," he said, "where are we—really?"

"We're in Tiburon, California, and I'm giving you the short happy life of Francis Macomber."

"Hemingway," said Runyan. To the surprise in her eyes, he added, "Prison library. Most of the guys wouldn't crack a book unless it hit 'em first, but I read a lot. For a few hours you could live someone else's life."

"We'll make this Fran*ces* Macomber—a.k.a. Louise Graham. I had two years at Rochester JC, was going to major in journalism at UofM, but I also had been dancing since I was five. That's what I meant about my folks not always being that way. Until I was a teen-ager, they doted on me. Then I started going out with boys and then started *staying* out, and . . ."

"For me it was getting drunk, getting into fights, having my buddies or the cops bring me home at three in the morning . . ."

"Anyway, I was a pretty good dancer . . . ballet, tap, jazz— they called it 'modern' then—and acrobatic."

She drank some wine. There was a far-off look in her eyes, and for the first time Runyan started to believe what she was telling him. She was really telling it to herself.

"Everybody kept saying I had what it takes to be a professional dancer. And for me being a professional meant glamor, easy money . . ."

"So you caught a bus to Vegas."

"You've heard this story before."

The waitress came around to ask them if they wanted coffee. They both did. She poured and withdrew.

"I was going to burn 'em up, knock 'em out . . ." Louise made an exaggerated sweeping motion with her hand. "ZOOM! Right to the top." She added cream and sugar to her coffee. "Instead, ZOOM! Right into a casting director's bed. Because Vegas is full of women who were told in *their* home towns that *they* had what it took. And who wanted the glamor and easy money just as much as I did . . ." Her voice rose slightly; her hands had closed into white-knuckled fists. "So I got into a show—but all it ever seemed to be was ostrich feathers and mesh stockings and bare boobs . . ."

He asked in an easy voice, "And a little favor for the management now and then?"

Louise gave a rueful little laugh. "You *have* heard this story before!" The animation died in her face. "All of a sudden I was at that line between amateur night and . . ."

"The first robbery I did was on a dare," said Runyan. "A

guy bet me fifty bucks I was afraid to climb up the side of an apartment building and steal somebody's stamp collection. I got my fifty bucks and he made ten thousand fencing the stamps. So I turned professional. I went over the line."

"I wasn't sure where the line was, but I knew I was over it. Since I couldn't stomach the thought of being a hooker, I started doing different kinds of favors, for a lot heavier people. Muling some grams here, once a kilo there . . . Flying to L.A. once a month to deposit skim money in a bank that *wasn't* connected . . ."

She drank coffee, checking her watch again as she did. She hadn't meant to tell him all this. She had been going to keep it light and full of laughs and ease her way back into his confidence, and suddenly she was into true confessions. And the hell of it was that she *wanted* to tell him all of it—or almost all.

"I finally realized that I was being a whore in a different way. And I wanted OUT—but they couldn't understand I just wanted to walk away, not turn snitch, not claim a reward, just . . . *hike*. And of course by then I knew a whole lot more about a whole lot more things and people than I wanted to. Than was *safe* to . . ." She looked over at him with sudden stunning realization. "Just like you. I wanted out from under and—"

"And you couldn't get out from under. We keep bouncing off one another, don't we?"

"But at least you have a choice. You can turn the diamonds over to Moyers and try to duck the others, or give them to the others and try to duck Moyers . . ."

"No," said Runyan. "I haven't recovered them yet." Before she could speak, he added, "How did you get out of it in Vegas?"

"A man. How else? He was there for a convention first, then kept coming back because he had gotten hooked on me . . ." She shrugged. "He was able to square it with those people—money or favors or maybe just convincing them that

I didn't want to blow any whistles, I never knew which. He wanted me to go with him, so I did. He set me up in a place."

She made a rueful face, and finished her coffee.

"A kept woman, a first for me—I sort of liked it. I'd slept with a lot of men, but I'd never had a real relationship with any of them. I guess I was naive. When things got tight financially for him, he wouldn't let me work to bring in some money. He just got nasty about what I cost to keep. Then, when I wanted to leave, he wouldn't let me do that, either . . ."

"Tell me how he kept you," said Runyan with a grin. "I sure haven't figured it out."

"That's easy—guilt. If it had just been force, I could have handled that. I've had a lot of practice. But it was—moral. He told me he was in real trouble, and that it was because of me. He said he needed to make a really big score to get even, and that I had to help him. He said I owed him."

"Did you?"

"I thought I did."

"What was the big score?"

She met his eyes with a steady gaze. "You."

"Make contact, get next to me, stick until I got the diamonds, then . . ."

She nodded. He turned his empty wine glass with his fingers for a long moment, then let out a long breath, nodded almost sadly, looked up and caught her gaze and held it.

"Only I didn't go get them when you thought I was going to, and you were gone when I got back." He paused for another long moment. "So why are you back now?"

Louise met his gaze levelly. "I'm on my own this time. For as long as you want me here." She stood up. "I'll be right back, darling."

Runyan watched her go out to the hallway where the restrooms and pay phone were located. He had a half-smile on his face. It slowly faded.

"Fool me once, shame on you. Fool me twice—shame on

me," he muttered to himself. He went quickly and quietly across the restaurant to lean against the pay phone partition.

"I don't have much time," Louise's voice was saying in low, urgent tones. "I'm back in, but he doesn't trust me yet. You won't be hearing anything from me for a while . . ."

Runyan, blank-faced, moved away as silently as he had come.

CHAPTER 19

Runyan woke with Louise's hair in his face; he was lying spoon-fashion against her back in his narrow bed, both of them nude under the covers. He could smell a lingering trace of her perfume. Why couldn't they just lie here the rest of the day, waking, dozing, loving . . . Memories of the overheard phone conversation the night before tried to crowd in, but he pushed them away. Just let him be unwary here, just for this time. Just . . .

He realized that for several moments her hips had been shifting against him, slyly, so he hadn't been consciously aware of being brought erect. He began gently rolling her left nipple between his fingers. She gave a sigh of contentment, reached down between her legs, and guided him into her waiting nest.

After almost a minute, her vaginal muscles began a rhythmic contraction around his rigid shaft; a few minutes later they climaxed exactly together, gently, lovingly, without a word having been spoken between them.

. . .

Louise turned right on Gough, running past the cold soaring spire of St. Mary's cathedral with the morning traffic's lemming rush for downtown. "Why do you have to see your parole officer? I thought you gave him your change of address."

"I did. But I have to leave the jurisdiction overnight to get the diamonds. I want permission ahead of time so they can't violate my parole."

Louise checked the rear-view mirror to get into the right lane so they wouldn't get sucked into the vortex of traffic funneling into the freeway entrance on Turk. She exclaimed, "Moyers is following us!"

"Moyers? How the hell did he . . ." Runyan interrupted himself, "Sharples! My parole officer! The son of a bitch sold Moyers my new address!"

"Why would your parole officer—"

"For the money." Runyan chuckled. "We'll just have to be creatively evasive when the time comes."

But when they pulled up in front of the regional parole office on South Van Ness, Runyan glanced across the sidewalk to the newspaper coin boxes. He took his hand quickly off the door handle. Looking across him, Louise could see the morning *Chronicle* headline:

LOAN COMPANY OFFICIAL MURDERED IN POSH PENTHOUSE APARTMENT

"If that headline's about who I think it is," said Runyan, "it changes everything. We're going to have to get out of town quicker than I thought, and we're going to *need* Moyers on our tail. Make sure he follows you, then don't lose him." He started out of the car. "I'll see you back at your hotel later."

He went across the sidewalk and into the building without a backward glance.

. . .

Sharples waited until Runyan had left the office, then put on his porkpie hat and went out. His secretary looked up angrily. She was always angry; knowing what about was a matter of nuance. He read this expression as one of angry surprise.

"You have another client in ten minutes," she snapped.

"I'll be back before then."

"If anyone calls, where have you gone?"

Though his mother had been dead for nearly four years, he was never going to get away from her; every woman in his life became her eventually. He left without replying. His secretary took a spiral notebook from her purse and made a notation; she was gathering evidence for a letter informing the Civil Service Commission that Mr. Sharples was not a good civil servant.

Sharples went out the back door to the pay phone in the adjacent gas station. Runyan could not see him from the bus stop; also, his secretary could not see him from her window. He knew all about her notations in her little spiral notebook; for the past six weeks, he had been keeping a similar record of *her* lapses, indulgences, and excesses.

Hi-Tech Electronics was on Larkin between Eddy and Ellis, a small, cramped, littered place much frequented by law enforcement people, both federal and state, from the government office buildings a couple of blocks away. Evidence obtained from illegal wire taps and room bugs, while not admissible in court, supplied a great many leads for evidence that *was* admissible.

High-Tech's owner/operator, a skinny man with horn-rimmed specs and long-fingered hands and his hair in Laurie Anderson spikes, was at his workbench when the phone rang. On the bench was a black box the size of a cigarette pack, with a magnet at one side and two small antennae extending out not more than an inch from the other side. He picked up the phone, listened for a moment, then handed it to his client, Moyers.

Sharples's voice, high-pitched with tension, said, "Runyan was in and said he was going camping in the Sierra for a week before he started to look for work. He wanted permission—"

"I told you I expected that," snapped Moyers impatiently.

"So I did what you . . . ah . . . suggested. I dated his permission letter tomorrow instead of today. But that means he can leave any time after midnight tonight . . ."

"I know what it means," said Moyers. "It means I'll have the son of a bitch when he makes his move."

The sparkling display windows faced Grant Avenue with tasteful arrangements of rings, necklaces, stones and earrings. Beside the inset entranceway was a discreet brass plaque:

GATIAN'S GEMSTONE GALAXY
Gemologists — Goldsmiths

As Runyan entered, he thought that Gatian had done well for himself since the robbery eight years ago. Everyone seemed to have done well except Runyan. And maybe Tenconi.

Gatian was frightened; he paced up and down his private office just barely controlling an impulse to wring his hands. Delarty, at the window, wore a sour look mixed with not a little impatience. On the desk was the same newspaper Runyan had seen, with the same headline visible.

"Take it easy, will you?" said Delarty. "Tenconi had a lot of enemies besides Runyan. Half the wops in North Beach probably are holding a candlelight parade now that he's—"

The door burst open and Runyan stormed in past Gatian's protesting secretary. His shirt was open halfway to his navel; there was a twitch to his hips and a lisp in his voice.

"Gatian sold me the ring for five thousand dollars last week," he exclaimed, "but my *friend* says it isn't worth a *penny* over three thousand, and I'm not going to be taken advantage of just because Gatian and I had a *moment* together . . ."

Delarty took his hand unobtrusively out from under his jacket. The flustered Gatian caught the movement. "Ah, Brenna, I'll . . . ah . . . take care of . . . um . . ."

He herded the distraught secretary out of the room as Runyan plunked himself down in the big impressive padded executive's swivel chair. He grabbed the edge of the big impressive executive's desk and spun himself around and around in the swivel chair as a kid might have done. He stopped himself by slamming a flattened palm down on the newspaper headline.

"You've got a problem, Gatian. Tenconi was a shit and Delarty here *is* a shit. But he steps into Tenconi's percentage so you two are partners." He gave an amused laugh. "Bambi and Godzilla." He tipped back in the swivel chair, and said to Delarty, "Your problem is stupidity. I'd like you for the hit on your partner, except that you aren't really smart enough to come up with that peephole idea . . ."

Blood suffused Delarty's already slightly choleric face. He took two steps forward and threw a roundhouse right at Runyan's jaw. Runyan snapped up a cocked leg so the fist thudded into the sole of his shoe. Delarty did a little dance about, nursing his skinned knuckles and breathing through his nose.

Runyan laughed. "You *are* smart enough," he said to Gatian, "but no guts." He came out from behind the desk. He looked from one to the other. "Which perhaps leaves Bambi and Godzilla together again, ridding the world of poor old Tenconi—and his claim to a percentage of the take."

"You could have worked it," said Delarty stubbornly.

"Sure I could have. But . . . kill me before I can recover the stones, you get nothing." He laughed aloud again. "Leave me alone, maybe you get dead."

Gatian, still nervous, began, "I'm sure we can work—"

"Or maybe it was Cardwell," suggested Runyan. "Maybe something snapped inside his head and he went after Tenconi." He grasped the doorknob and turned it, not quite pulling the door open. "Or maybe it *was* one of you, working independently, not telling the other how you were going to do in old Tenconi. I'd keep an eye on each other if I were you."

Then he opened the door and slipped through, closing it firmly behind him. Delarty glanced almost accusingly across the room at Gatian—and was startled to meet an equally hostile glare from him.

From Gatian's, Runyan went to the nearest medical office in the phone book and waited until a doctor could see him. He explained that he was involved in a complicated business deal that he found impossible to put out of his mind, so he was having difficulty getting to sleep at night. The doctor gave him a prescription.

Forcing himself to consider only the necessity Louise's phone call seemed to dictate, he had the prescription filled at the drugstore on the corner. Then he went in search of Louise, feeling guilty but more secure.

CHAPTER 20

The day was an education for Louise. She was seeing a new Runyan, perhaps Runyan as he had been before the destructive years in San Quentin. He was funny and loose and a little reckless, turning up at the hotel and kissing her in the lobby where she'd been waiting for his arrival.

"Let's go spend some money," he said.

They spent it in a mountaineering shop, renting or buying boots, jackets, a two-man tent, a Coleman pressure lantern and fold-up stove, Gold Line rope, pitons, chocks, and a pair of odd-looking clamplike things which he called Jumar ascenders. Louise reached for her credit card, but Runyan said he had money from his brother.

She turned away, looking almost embarrassed, as the clerk tallied up the charges. He was a husky kid wearing a T-shirt which showed the tracks of climbing boots on his chest, one foot going each way, with the legend underneath, *JUST A LITTLE BIT CRAZY.*

"Where are you climbing?" he asked.

"Yosemite."

"It's great this time of year." Louise returned to stand close with an arm around Runyan as he counted out the money. "Which climbs are you doing?"

"I thought we'd warm up on Monday Morning Slab, then try the Royal Arches," said Runyan.

"Which ascent?"

Runyan grinned. "The easiest one."

As they piled the back seat of Louise's car high with their gear, she kept looking for Moyers. And kept not seeing him. She finally mentioned it to Runyan.

"He's got other things to do."

"How does he know we won't ditch him again?"

"He knows where you're staying, and Sharples dated my permission letter to go camping in the Sierra for tomorrow instead of today. What does that tell you?"

"Nothing," said Louise promptly.

"That Moyers *told* him to postdate it. Because Moyers knows we aren't *just* going to go camping—"

"I don't know that," said Louise suspiciously.

"Well, we aren't. So Moyers will make sure we don't ditch him at the vital moment."

"That doesn't bother you?"

"I wouldn't have it any other way."

He must have been an excellent thief, she thought scrutinizing this new Runyan. His mind was always moving, leaping ahead, figuring angles, foreseeing contingencies. Except he hadn't foreseen the unexpected arrival of a guard.

"Well, are you going to tell me about it?"

"Why spoil your fun?" he said, and wouldn't say another word on the subject.

They spent the rest of the afternoon at the Department of Motor Vehicles on Fell Street. Runyan read the booklet, took the written test—100 out of 100—and then the driving test. He was issued his temporary license.

They were back to her hotel by ten o'clock. The sodium

lights of the underground garage gave the cold concrete a golden, almost sensuous glow by which they embraced and kissed until both were slightly dizzy. They went off to the elevators with their arms around one another, so relaxed that their steps were unsteady as a drunk's.

"We'll be making an early start in the morning," he warned.

"And an even earlier start tonight."

"We're going to get something straight between us?"

Her muted, silvery laughter followed them through the doorway marked ELEVATOR TO MOTEL.

After nearly a minute, a car door slammed, and casual footsteps echoed hollowly in the empty garage. Moyers strolled past the backs of parked cars until he reached Louise's. His hand brought the little black cigarette-pack-size box out of his pocket; he bent quickly and reached in under the rear bumper. There was a muted clank as the magnet on the side of the box grabbed the metal of the bumper behind the rubber sheath.

He strolled back to his car and pulled out of the garage. He was pretty sure they weren't going to try any tricks like taking off at one minute after midnight, because Runyan would think his change of address had taken care of Moyers's ability to find him again. But just in case, another night in the car. He was used to all-night stakeouts from years of practice.

Runyan might be a hell of a thief; but he was pitiful going up against a professional like Moyers, whose job it was to keep tabs on people who didn't want tabs kept on them.

The low steady beeping noise which had lulled him to sleep turned to a steady electronic whine. Moyers sat up straight and checked his watch. Nine a.m. An intermittent beep meant the car was motionless; the whine indicated the car had started moving.

There was a square black radio receiver/viewing screen attached to his dashboard. Its glowing red sighting bar was steady. The Toyota appeared, Runyan behind the wheel, and

Louise beside him. Probably got a driver's license the day before, along with all of that camping equipment. He wouldn't take a chance on a parole violation by driving without one.

Moyers stayed where he was until the Toyota was lost in the traffic ahead; then he pulled out, secure in the knowledge that the transmitter would guide him.

Runyan drove west through the Avenues on Geary Boulevard, toward the Cliff House and Ocean Beach. They swung down past the crumbling fake rock face of Sutro Heights in the grey chill morning fog, then followed the Great Highway south. The Pacific boomed off to their right, occasionally visible over the sea wall and between the shifting pale sand dunes. Louise had the heater on and Runyan had to use the windshield wipers.

"It ought to burn off about eleven," said Runyan.

He pulled off parallel to the storm fence that helped hold the dunes back from the highway. Wind-whipped sand stung Louise's face and gritted between her teeth as he led her up to a point above the sea. In the surf far below, the blackened ribs of a wrecked sailing ship formed an oval just visible a foot or two above the sand.

"I read about this in Q," Runyan called to her above the moan of the wind. "An old British sailing ship from the mid-eighteen-hundreds. Beached herself here and just rotted away."

"Couldn't they salvage it?" she yelled.

"Not in those days. And I guess the storms covered her with sand so everybody forgot about her until last year, when the storms finally uncovered her again."

The wreckage seemed to have some special meaning for him, but Louise, her teeth almost chattering until the heater took over again, was glad when they returned to the car.

"Will they salvage it now?" she asked.

"Naw. A year or two, the storms'll cover her up again, and they'll forget about her for another hundred years or so." He looked over at her. "I always wanted to go diving in the lagoon at Truk atoll in the Pacific. A whole fleet went down there in World War Two. It would be something to see."

He felt her eyes on him, turned and caught her questing gaze. He shrugged, almost sheepishly.

"One of the great moments of my life, I must have been ten or so, was when I realized I didn't have to be a judge like my father, and didn't have to live in Portland my whole life." He paused, shrugged again. "From as far back as I can remember, all I wanted was to be free—away, on my own . . . But . . ."

"But 'they' wouldn't let you?"

"*I* wouldn't let me. I always fucked it up."

"Yeah," said Louise, thinking of her own life, "tell me about it."

They both laughed.

The highway left the sea and joined Skyline Boulevard by Lake Merced. Patches of anemic blue were starting to show through the fog: joggers huffed and puffed along the running paths around the lake. At Daly City, Highway One swept down to Pacifica and the sea once again. Oddly, the ticky-tacky houses faced each other rather than the ocean, as if the remarkable view had been too much for the developers to take.

"Did you come this way the night . . . *that* night?"

Runyan laughed. "I know somebody else asking that question about now."

Louise looked involuntarily around, but there was no way to tell whether a car was following them in the freeway traffic.

Runyan stopped at Shelter Cove for a bucket of the Colonel's best, with rolls and fries and slaw and cokes. A few miles further on, he pulled over into one of the numerous view areas which flanked the highway.

"A *picnic*?" she asked in disbelief.

"Man does not live by diamonds alone."

"You're just having yourself a hell of a time, aren't you?"

"I'm trying," he said with great delight.

The sun was strong now, the fog gone; suddenly a picnic on the beach seemed a good idea. They started down a steep earth path through the greasewood and manzanita toward the sheltered triangle of sand far below.

Excitement tugged at Moyers as he eased into an unpaved pull-off with a good view of the rugged coastline ahead. He dictated into his recorder, "Subject vehicle has stopped at eleven-fifty-one a.m. at a view area on Highway One approximately five miles south of Rockaway Beach."

He got out, binoculars in hand. Runyan could have come this far south that night, and still gotten back up to Marin in time to go off the freeway and eventually into San Quentin. But he couldn't be so goddamn gone on the woman that he was just going to take her right to the place where the diamonds were stashed, could he?

At the row of boulders left over when the road had been scraped out of the face of the cliffs, he used the powerful glasses. The Toyota was empty in the view area a quarter of a mile ahead. He scanned down toward the beach below. So suddenly that it startled him, two tiny dots of scrambling color sprang full-size to life as Runyan and Louise, just going in a rush together, hand-in-hand, down the final steep bit of trail to the soft sand of the cove's beach. He could even read the familiar red Kentucky Fried Chicken logo on their big white paper bag.

That explained the stop at Shelter Cove—a goddamned picnic! And him without a damned thing in the car to eat. He raised the glasses again. They were spreading out their food in the shelter of a big driftwood log. Runyan was clever, he had to give him that. If the diamonds had been hidden here, this was a recon—which Louise would think was just a picnic.

Refresh his memory in broad daylight, then come back here at night to get the diamonds. Yeah. Damned clever.

But not as clever as the man who had fastened the bug to the inside of his back bumper. Moyers permitted himself a self-satisfied stretch, then raised the glasses for another look.

CHAPTER 21

Louise rummaged with greasy fingers in the bucket for the final piece. She took a big crunching bite and gestured with the maimed thigh as she chewed. "No diamonds stashed here?"

Runyan's gaze followed her gesture around the little cove. Gulls wheeled and keened overhead. Down at the surfline, sandpipers dressed like tuxedoed dandies chased a receding breaker back toward the ocean on spindly legs.

"Maybe no diamonds stashed anywhere."

"Why don't I believe you?"

"Why doesn't anyone believe me?"

His tone made the movement of her jaws slow for a moment as she weighed whether he was serious or not. Then she laughed and stood up and brushed the front of her jeans.

"You'd be in a mess if there *really* weren't any diamonds."

Runyan stood up also, doing a lousy W. C. Fields imitation. "That I would, m'dear," he said, "that I would indeed."

They stuffed all the junk into the Colonel's bucket and

started back toward the path, their shoes sinking deep into the soft pale sand at each step. There was a momentary flash of light, not repeated, from the bluff a quarter of a mile back.

"Why are you grinning, monkey?" Louise demanded.

"What is it that guy says on television? 'I love it when a plan comes together'?"

Going up the steep narrow winding path was easier on the knees than coming down, but it took Louise's breath away almost instantly. "That doesn't *have* to be Moyers up on the bluff with a pair of binoculars."

"It doesn't make sense any other way. He had Sharples date my permission to leave for today instead of yesterday so he would have time to put a bug on your car." Louise noted enviously that he wasn't even breathing hard. "I *hope* he had time to put a bug on your car. Otherwise we're in big trouble."

When Moyers's headlights swept across the sign which read ENTERING YOSEMITE NATIONAL PARK, the gate was untended. He swung down a long curve flanked by tumbled grey granite, and was on the valley floor. Even with the windows closed he could hear the clatter of fast brown water over the rocks of a nearby riverbed.

Runyan had driven up over the coast range at Half Moon Bay, had crossed the Bay on California 92, then had used the Interstates to Manteca to pick up California 120 directly here. Obviously going to camp in the park for a day or two, making it look good. Probably also trying to make sure nobody was on his tail. Moyers chuckled silently to himself. The homing device on the dash emitted its thin unvarying whine.

Still early enough to call Vegas when he got in. And to get some supper. God, he was starving, he was glad he'd had his office make reservations ahead. He'd spent a Labor Day weekend at the Ahwanee Lodge with his then-wife almost 15 years ago; alone was better, he wouldn't have to keep faking awed reactions to the mountains. A mountain was just rocks piled up too high, and never would be anything else to him.

Camp Four was called the Zoo, because the serious rock climbers stayed there. Louise had never camped out in her life, but Runyan set up their two-man tent and made supper on the one-burner Coleman stove with admirable efficiency. Bacon, onion, and garlic sauteed in a saucepan, two cans of baked beans and half a bottle of syrup dumped in for the last few minutes. They ate it all.

The two climbers at the next numbered pad had started a fire, so Runyan got out the bottle of red wine they'd bought. He stepped to the edge of their fire and raised the freshly-opened bottle by the neck interrogatively, totally at his ease here, with none of the tensions and quick suspicions she had come to think of as part of his basic nature.

"Hey, great, man!" exclaimed one of them.

It was cold enough that all four were wrapped in their heavy down jackets. Runyan took a slug of wine and handed the bottle to Louise. She drank and passed it on to the one who'd spoken to them. He was a man in his early twenties who talked incessantly and smoked relentlessly. His name was Steve.

His partner was in his mid-thirties, with piercing eyes and thin floppy black hair and a pair of newish jeans and positively filthy tennis shoes. He wordlessly saluted Runyan with the bottle and drank deeply.

"He's Italian," said Steve. "Wherever there's a mountain he speaks the language. Except English." Steve held out thumb and forefinger a scant quarter-inch apart. "I speak a little Spanish so we don't have any problems."

"Giovanni," said the Italian suddenly.

Runyan leaned forward. He pointed to his chest. "*Soy* Runyan." He indicated Louise. "*Está es mi mujer Luisa.*"

"Ah. *Luisa.*" Giovanni grinned and leaned forward gallantly to kiss Louise's hand. Then he shook enthusiastically with Runyan.

Louise said to Runyan, "Where did you learn Spanish?"

"We had a lot of Latinos in the joint."

There were so many facets to Runyan that she didn't know about. The thought almost numbingly and suddenly struck her: I am in love with this man. Screw everything else, I'm in love with him.

Runyan turned back to Giovanni. *"Estéban dice que usted es de Italia."*

"Sí. De Ticino. Es la parte Italiana de los Alpes. He estado viajando durante un año, escalaro por todo el mundo."

"¿Donde están las montañas chingonas?"

"En el Rusia. Los Urales. Son las más peñosas y magníficas. Mejorísimas que los Alpes."

The firelight flickered across their faces, making their features ruddy and dusky by turns; the bottle was making its circle again. Runyan turned back to her.

"Giovanni is from the Italian Alps. He's been travelling and climbing for a year, all over the world. He says the rockwork in the Urals, in Russia, is much better than the Alps."

Louise made a gesture around. "How do you like Yosemite?"

"Aquí se encuentran las más bonitas de todas las montañas," said Giovanni.

"The most beautiful," said Runyan.

Louise made a departing gesture with her hands. "From here—where?"

"El Perú. Ya, si yo tuviera el dinero por un boleto, a India," said Giovanni. *"Las Himalayas."*

Runyan had asked Steve, "Which climbs have you guys done?"

"The nose of El Cap. The Northwest Buttress and the North Ridge of Half Dome . . ."

Runyan nodded, said to Louise, "Did you get that? Peru? The Himalayas?"

"Didn't he say something about *A Passage to India*?"

Runyan laughed. "He's going to India to climb the Himalayas if he can find the money for his passage."

Steve was saying, "Tomorrow we're doing the transverse to Lost Arrow. If you guys want to come along . . ."

Runyan grinned and shook his head.

"Out of practice?"

"Amateurs." Steve gave him an appraising look, not accepting that, recognizing one of his own, but Runyan added, "Monday Morning Slab tomorrow. That's us."

When the fire died down and the bottle went dry, they broke up, Steve and Giovanni hitting the sack, Runyan and Louise walking over to the store: Runyan had to make a phone call.

"About the diamonds?" she asked.

"Of course."

"Can I listen in?"

"Of course not."

Camping areas made little puddles of light in the darkness. There was no moon, but the air was so clear that the sky was almost pale with the stipplings of the Milky Way. When Louise blew out she could see her breath.

"You're just sore because I was making time with Giovanni."

"He tried to buy you," said Runyan in perfect seriousness.

"Tried to . . ." Then she realized he was putting her on and laughed. She didn't know when she had felt so happy. She wanted it to go on forever. "If Moyers did follow us, where do you suppose he is right now?"

Probably the Ahwanee Lodge—one of the big old national park hotels built by the CCC back in the 'thirties. Really beautiful—hand-laid stone fireplaces and formal dining rooms and carved hardwood . . ."

"Can we see?" she exclaimed.

"Better not, he might catch us poking around. We need him playing our game, not the other way around."

"Just what is our game?"

"Rock climbing," he said.

She looked over at him in the starlit darkness. "Sometimes I wish I knew what was *really* going on in that head of yours."

The room was spacious but simple, hardwood floors and knotty pine walls and a lot of blankets on the double bed. On the floor beside it the homing transceiver from the car pinged intermittently to itself. Moyers, on the phone, waited through the clicks and windy silences of his credit-card call until Stark, the Las Vegas detective, answered the phone.

"I've got a little more for you on her," Stark said.

"I hoped you might."

"She was getting a little salty, they were afraid they couldn't trust her any more, so they tossed a scare into her," said Stark's heavy voice. He stressed all his syllables equally, like the computer-generated voice of Information. "The usual, we're gonna toss acid in your face—like that. She bought it and lit a shuck out of town, which was all they wanted anyway."

"Alone?"

"You kidding?" Stark gave a grating chuckle. "She already had a visiting fireman lined up, panting to play house with her."

"Tell me about him," said Moyers.

As he listened, he unconsciously nodded to himself several times. Then he started grinning. Just what he'd thought but hadn't dared to hope. It was all going to work out. He had Runyan just where he wanted him.

On the canvas floor was a French four-in-one handtorch which cast a pale white fluorescent glow over the interior of the tent. When Runyan came crouching through the zippered flap, Louise was already inside, kneeling half-undressed on their double sleeping bag. God, he wanted her! Looking at her smooth bare shoulders, the delicate ivory slope of her brassiered breasts, he knew he could never get enough of her.

"Can you believe I've never slept in one of these?"

"What makes you think you're going to sleep tonight?" he leered.

Then he remembered what Taps Turner had said on the phone: It was set for two nights from now in L.A. The plane would be at the airfield from 10:30 on. He turned quickly away, on the pretext of zipping up the tent flap.

He'd told Taps he'd be there. Alone. Goddammit, why couldn't it be simple? Why had he had to overhear that damned phone call? Why had Louise had to make it? Why . . .

Louise's hot, naked body landed on his back. Runyan tumbled sideways onto the sleeping bag, breaking her grip, his gloom of a moment before dispelled.

"You've led me on long enough," she exclaimed in baritone tones. "Now I'm taking what you deny me!"

"Get away from me!" he squeaked in a girlish falsetto. "I'm not that kind of girl!"

"Then why are you taking off your pants?" she demanded suspiciously.

"I thought I'd slip into something more comfortable."

Louise switched off the torch. "Hi," she said in the dark, "my name is Comfortable."

A few minutes later, Runyan said, rather breathlessly, "It certainly is."

CHAPTER 22

Monday Morning Slab, near the base of the north face of Glacier Point, was an upended triangular plate of granite 400 feet high. Moyers sat on a fallen tree a quarter of a mile away, using his binoculars to bring up Runyan and Louise. The early morning sun cast their shadows long and thin across the carpeted pine needles at the foot of the massive slab.

Runyan, with that remarkable combination of daring and caution which marks the skilled climber, scrambled up a pitch like a monkey going up a tree. No wonder the man had ended up a cat burglar; what else could he have done?

Moyers switched to Louise, watched her with conditioned, almost indifferent lust—and a great feeling of power. He knew enough to make her get out of it any time he wanted, leaving Runyan out there naked and alone. Except for Moyers.

Back to Runyan. He had driven a piton into a crack in the

rock and clipped a carabiner to it; through this was run the safety rope which trailed down the rock to Louise. She was still on the ground a dozen yards below, looking up, shading her eyes with her hands, the safety rope running down from Runyan, under her backside, and up to be tied around her waist.

Runyan gave it a healthy jerk. Since it was wrapped around her butt, she was slammed painfully against her rock.

Moyers chuckled as he watched her yell angrily up at him. He lowered the glasses. Giving him hell. He'd like to give her something, all right, when all of this was over. But right now, TCB, as the hookers said—Take Care of Business.

He unclipped his canteen awkwardly from his belt, drank half the contents straight down, lowered it, and wiped his mouth on his sleeve. Tough work, this rock climbing. When he raised the binoculars again, Runyan was far up the face on a ledge, with the safety line tied off around a rock.

Moyers found Louise below, carefully climbing upward, searching out toe- and finger-holds, her face red and sweating and contorted with effort. Do the bitch good, he thought with surprising bitterness. He hadn't forgotten how easily she'd given him the slip at the airport.

Of course she was a pro. Running casino skim to L.A. for laundering, being nice to important clients from time to time for the pit boss; then, when things went sour, cold-bloodedly picking out a protector to get her out of Vegas. A protector, as last night's phone conversation with Stark had confirmed, whom Moyers had seen sneaking out of the hotel after the shooting attempt on Runyan. A lethal lady to fall for.

In his binoculars, Louise was just below the ledge. Her foot slipped, her knee bashed the rock face painfully. He could see her yelping her pain, but Runyan's grip on the safety rope kept her from sliding. She got a hand on the ledge, he caught her wrist and helped her up.

Moyers lowered the glasses and turned away. They were

safely up on the rock face for the next couple of hours; plenty of time to snoop their car and tent and duffel bag and make sure he left no trace of his visit. He was really getting into this. It was all downhill for him from here.

An hour later, Louise was standing under a steep overhang with the safety line hanging down from it to a loose coil at her feet. Her neck was stiff and her eyes burned from hours of looking up into the sun. Her body prickled with the salt crust of drying sweat; her inner thighs stung from chafing. All her muscles ached. She just knew her face was blotchy and her hair a mess from the pitiless sun. This was *fun*?

Runyan rappelled down the rope from above to land lightly beside her. He grinned. "How you making it?"

"Fine," she snapped irritably.

He unsnapped from the safety line, went over to rummage in their black nylon haul sack. "I know this is just easy practice stuff, but we have to get ready for—"

"I'll keep it up as long as you, damn you!" she exclaimed.

Runyan looked at her in surprise. He held the odd-looking things he had called ascenders or something like that.

"Hey, I'm sorry, sweetie," he said, mistaking the source of her irritation. "This isn't a putdown or anything..." He started to adjust the ascenders on the hanging safety line, one above the other at about head height. "I'm so out of shape for climbing I don't want to take you on a real rock face until I'm sure I can handle it." He gestured at the safety line. "You remember these, don't you? Jumar ascenders?"

He was just being dense on purpose, to goad her, talking over his shoulder without even turning around. Totally frazzled, she snapped, "Do you really think I *care*, Runyan? I've barked my shin, I'm dying of thirst..."

"These can be used for horizontal traverse, but..."

"—blisters on my heels and rope burns on my hands—"

"... but climbers usually use them to climb ropes belayed from above on overhung rock faces like this one."

"—and you want to talk to me about something called *Jumar ascenders*?"

Each Jumar had a rope sling hanging from it. Runyan stepped a foot into each sling, turned and grinned at her. "They're so great because you can just walk right up a rope with them."

He did, hand above hand, each knee flexing as the Jumar from which that sling depended moved, thus literally walking straight up the line and out of her vision.

Louise found herself stepping back a few paces, even as she fumed, squinting up into the sunlight to see how he did it. Damn, her neck was sore. But he was right: Those Jumars were pretty neat things.

They sat facing one another on top of the massive flake of granite in the red scorch of dying sun.

"Red sky at night, sailors delight," said Runyan.

He offered her the canteen and she drank sparingly, small sips which let her savor the cool nectar running down inside her throat. Runyan put the canteen back on his belt without taking any himself; his water discipline was remarkable.

"Is it always like this? Climbing?"

He shook his head. "Usually it's a lot more fun."

"I didn't mean that."

She looked out and away, up the incredible valley the retreating glaciers had casually sliced through the middle of the Sierra during the last ice age. Deep purple peaks thrust up against the sunset which had retreated from scarlet to faded rose and delicate grey.

"I mean, this close to—"

She stopped, seeking words to express the inexpressible. She ached all over, she couldn't count the scrapes and nicks and cuts and bruises on the outward angles of all her joints, she was tired and hungry and sunburned—and she had never felt so good.

"I just feel . . . as if it were all made for me."

"Just a little something I had God lay on for you."

"Thanks, Runyan." She leaned forward and they kissed.

She was still thinking in superlatives as she took her shower, even though it was just a trickle of cold water from a rusted-out showerhead in the ladies' facility near Camp Four. She rubbed herself red with the rough towel, scrubbed her hair halfway dry with it, realizing her mind was made up.

She'd always acted quickly on urges and impulses, even on intuitions, and her feelings about Runyan were more than intuition. God help her, more than infatuation. But she also always thought of herself as an intensely loyal person.

Now she realized that loyalty carried too far ceased being a virtue and became cowardice. So she had to do it. Tonight. A clean break with the past, no turning back because there would be nothing left to turn back to.

After supper, Runyan sat on a rock by the fire and she sat on the ground beside him, her forearms crossed on his knee, looking into the flames. It was a much warmer night, or she was getting used to it. Sap made the green wood crack and spit showers of sparks. Around them but somehow at a distance other climbers sat around other fires, their voices and bursts of laughter carried like swarms of fireflies on the gusts of warm wind.

"Tomorrow?" she asked.

"Royal Arches."

She looked at him over her shoulder. "Should I be scared?"

"You'll be fine." He put a hand on her shoulder for a moment. "You were great today."

He poured red wine into two styrofoam cups and handed her one. They raised the cups in a mutual toast.

"To crime," said Louise.

At the same instant, Runyan said, "To love."

They drank quickly, each mildly disconcerted by the other's toast. Louise put aside her empty cup and scrambled almost abruptly to her feet. Runyan, in the act of pouring more wine, looked up at her in surprise.

"I'm going over and get an ice cream cone." She was glad of the shielding darkness that hid her expression. "Want me to bring you one back?"

Runyan merely shook his head, smiling dreamily after her. He sipped wine from the styrofoam cup, and fought a mighty battle in his mind. Love made him want to sit right there staring at the embers of the fire; survival tried to drag him to his feet. It was a wretched feeling. How in God's name had the old people he saw walking hand-in-hand down suburban streets gotten through it all to reach that point in their lives still together? What was their secret that he didn't know?

Runyan stood, threw his cup into the coals. It hissed and blackened and shrivelled. Her betrayal of him forced him to be a betrayer also—of himself, of her, of the facts he knew. Why did he need her so? Was this the ultimate irony: that she might be the one against whom he would have to defend himself?

He went silently after her into the darkness. Even as he ran he kept hoping, thinking, I'm wrong, all she wants over at the store is an ice cream cone.

But she was spotlit inside the phone booth, feeding her coins into the prim little mechanical mouth. He moved quickly and with little noise through the foliage behind the booth, his hands guiding the small branches back to their original positions individually. He was so close that when she spoke it was as if into his ear.

"It's me," her voice said into the phone. "I've always played straight with you so I'm playing straight now. This is the last phone call you'll be getting. I'm dropping out."

Runyan started to ease his way almost blindly back through the foliage. He couldn't stand listening to her. He couldn't stand spying on her. He needn't have been here. She was not a betrayer. He was.

Louise was saying, "Well think what you want, buster, it isn't the money . . ." She listened, spoke again, her voice edged with tears. "I tried, goddamn you, I really tried! But all you ever wanted was a piece of me, not the whole package. I can't live like that any more. I need some absolutes . . ."

CHAPTER 23

Louise's boot turned over a rock; it clattered loudly in the dry stream bed along which she followed Runyan. She shivered with the cold despite the heavy coil of Gold Line rope slung bandolier-fashion over one shoulder and across her chest. The icy dawn air offered no suggestion of the day's heat to come.

Runyan, loaded down with their haul sack and all of the climbing gear, gestured up at the towering rock face which stretched a sickening 3,000 feet above them. His breath went up in white puffs.

"I'll be leading the climb, all you have to do is follow. Just remember that you'll be roped in, and that if anything happens, I'll be set to take the strain."

Her mouth felt suddenly dry, full of cotton. This wasn't like Monday Morning Slab. "You talk too much," she snapped.

Runyan didn't answer. He was concentrated, focused, thrusting last night from his mind, thrusting away everything but the mechanics of the climb.

Four hours later, his groping hand found the edge of a narrow rock ledge. He levered himself up, turned, and sat down with his feet dangling over eternity. The tops of the pines were so far below now that they had lost all individual definition and were just a rich green spiky carpet. He snubbed off the safety line to a bolt some earlier climber had left sunk in the rock.

"Off belay!" he called down to where Louise waited on a similar ledge a hundred feet below. He took a sparing swig of water from the canteen. He was starting to steam in the warming midmorning sun.

"Tension!" came Louise's distant response.

Runyan immediately took up the slack on the safety rope by drawing it through the bolt until it was taut but not tight. He held the line in his hands as she started up, feeling her as a deep sea fisherman will feel the marlin delicately mouthing his bait fifty fathoms below. As she climbed, he kept drawing in the rope to maintain that even tension which gives the climber a feeling of confidence and thus reduces the chance of accident.

Louise carefully followed the taut rope up the nearly vertical face, using the handholds and bolts and chocks which Runyan had left set for her. All her energies were concentrated on the climbing; no room left for anything else. Every movement of the hand, every placement of the foot, had to be thought out beforehand, then performed without hesitation and with absolute precision. Dancing had never required such precision.

Her jitters were gone, and the residual stiffness from yesterday's practice climbs had long since worked itself out of her muscles. She was loving it; even the sweat which bathed her body and stung her eyes was given a sensual quality by the edge of danger always present.

She paused to clear the chock she had just passed; the downward pressure caused by the weight of a climber's body was what wedged chocks so firmly into fissures in the rock; by pulling upward, she reversed that pressure and freed it. She clipped it, jangling, with the others on her belt, and looked up to seek out the next handhold. She was a hell of a lot better at this than she had been even an hour before.

They ate lunch on another ledge nearly a thousand feet further from the valley floor, Spam sandwiches washed down with tepid canteen water. From here the hotel, the camp grounds, the road, even the river and the forests far below them just weren't relevant any more.

"Like all the shit one gets himself into," said Runyan.

He so precisely voiced Louise's own thoughts, that she said, "What?" in a rather startled voice.

He swung an arm to indicate everything below. Louise nodded, then suddenly clutched his arm, galvanized by an impossibly wide flat rakish black shadow drifting far out from the cliffs.

"Golden eagle," said Runyan. It wheeled in the sunlight; a wash of pale gold flashed momentarily on the back of its neck.

"He gets to live like this all the time," she mused.

Runyan looked over at her. The wind, midday hot, tugged at their clothes and riffled their hair. He nodded.

"I love you," he said in a voice muffled by the last of the sandwich he was chewing.

She whirled to stare at him. "What did you say?"

Runyan licked his fingers and wiped them on his trousers as he pushed himself back from the lip and stood up.

"We'd better get going."

"*What did you say, damn you?*"

"That we have to get cracking if we don't want to spend the night slung in hammocks halfway up this mother."

"You're a real bastard, you know that, Runyan?"

"I'm glad me poor mither isn't here to hear you say that," he said in a broad Irish brogue.

They both laughed, and the moment passed. Runyan

clipped one of the carabiners from his belt to a bolt driven into the rock behind the ledge. Louise looked up, craning back a bit trying to see what was above them. It looked like there was nothing above them. A vertical rock face without the slightest sign of any hand or footholds. She had learned enough in this long day to recognize that.

"I hate to mention it," she said, "but where are we supposed to go from here?"

Runyan was tying one end of the Gold Line through the carabiner. He jerked it, hung on it with his full weight. He nodded and came erect. "Sideways," he said.

Louise looked horizontally along the rock face. There were handholds, all right, but they looked pretty scary to her. She felt a sudden hollowness in the pit of her stomach.

"Sideways," she said in a flat disbelieving voice.

"After I do a little maneuver called a pendulum," he said. "It looks a lot more spectacular than it is." He tested the rope again, then began slinging it around him, getting ready to rappel down it. "What it really is, it's a hell of a lot of fun."

Moyers, full of a good lunch from the hotel dining room, belched almost delicately as he picked his way up the dry stream bed toward the frightening sheer rock face which one of the waiters had called the Royal Arches. He could see nothing resembling arches in the mound of granite rising ahead of him. Neither could he see anything resembling Runyan and Louise.

He began glassing the rock face with his binoculars. Suddenly Louise leaped out at him. She was alone on a rock ledge, peering carefully down.

Down?

The roving glasses found Runyan a hundred feet below, lashed to the far end of a line fastened somehow beside Louise. Runyan was leaning back away from the rock, almost out at a right angle to it. Even as Moyers picked him out, he turned to his right and began *running* along the face of the cliff. It was the damndest thing Moyers had ever seen, and the most unexpected. He could not have been more surprised if Runyan had spread his arms and started to fly.

At the far end of the arc controlled by the length of the safety line, Runyan whirled nimbly and began running in the other direction as fast as he could, out to the other extremity of the arc in a sort of giant pendulum. At the end of this run, he stretched as far as he could, and tried to jam his hand into a crack in the rock face. He missed by scant inches.

As his momentum failed, Runyan whirled and started his run back the other way again, bounding across the face of the mountain as if he possessed seven-league boots. At the far end he returned, running faster, stretching further—and managed to jam his fingers into the crack and hold himself there against the backswing gravity. He had made it.

Moyers lowered the binoculars. Sweat was standing on the back of his neck. He didn't like the bastard, but he had to admit that had been something to see. Without the glasses, the two climbers were merely flecks of colored confetti against the grey rock and black shadow of the cliff face.

He took his cassette recorder from his pocket and said, "Subject is attempting a climb on the Royal Arches. I am told this is usually an overnight effort. I will continue to observe the subject as I am able to do so."

Runyan was safely on the mountain until the next day. Which meant, Moyers thought, that he had lost all options except the one Moyers had chosen for him.

The westering sun pushed heavy shadows out across the valley floor over half a mile below. The wind was cooler, with a hint of evening in it, as Runyan worked his way across the forehead of a great slanting expanse of bald rock, an "aid climb" using chocks and pitons. Above him he could see the Jungle, as the foliage which rimmed the crown of Royal Arches like a receding hairline was called. He crawled up the last few feet, stood up, and yelled down at Louise.

"Off belay."

Seventy-five feet below the balding crown of rock, Louise began her traverse, following the safety line along the trail of chocks and pitons Runyan had left for her. Her movements were now quick and sure despite her fatigue; she had come a long way figuratively as well as literally during that day.

Runyan, standing in the shrubbery at the edge of the Jungle, tended her safety line without thought, kept the tension on automatically; his hands were busy but his mind was free.

He had told her he loved her. Unexpectedly: It had just popped out. He did love her. But did he trust her? What would he do tonight when they got back down? Everything that had happened to him in the past eight years—intensified since his release from San Quentin—passed one ineluctable message to his brain: Don't trust anyone. Especially someone who has already betrayed you once.

But last night . . .

Hell, last night she could have heard a crackle in the brush, could have guessed you were there, and said what she knew you wanted to hear.

So what? You didn't want the fucking diamonds, even when you thought they still existed. You don't want the money from the robbery you're planning with Taps. You don't want anything in this world except your freedom. And Louise.

Would there ever be any freedom with a woman you weren't sure you could trust?

Would there ever be any freedom without her?

"I love you," he said aloud. Through his mind passed a line from an old Tin Pan Alley tune: *There, I said it again.*

Just then he heard the labored sounds of her approach. The slack of the safety line was neatly coiled beside him; he didn't remember doing it. She appeared on the bald forehead of rock, walking herself up with the aid of the safety line. She had a big smile on her face. Jesus, what a woman he had found! He reached out and gave her a hand up.

How could he have had any doubts?

"Congratulations," he said. "Half the experienced people I used to climb with couldn't have made Royal Arches in one day."

Louise was too exhausted to give him more than a bushed smile. They sat down side-by-side on a windfall tree at the edge of the Jungle, swinging their legs and staring out over the view. Louise took the canteen and drank greedily.

She finally lowered it to say, "God was feeling good when he made these mountains."

"And when he made you."

She looked quickly over at him, caught by an intensity of emotion in his voice she had never heard before; but he was looking out over the incredible twilight vistas of the valley.

"This is what I missed in prison. *Really* missed."

"Then why become a thief?"

"Adventure," he said. "Excitement. Beating the system. But then it changes. All of a sudden, money isn't what you get any more. It's what you *have*." He looked at her, something close to pain in his eyes. "And you *want* it, because you've started living in a way you can support *only* by stealing."

"Or by compromising," said Louise, her thoughts turning inward. "Compromising until there's nothing of *you* left except the marrow in your bones."

Runyan nodded. "I was a thief for six years before they caught me. Always worked alone, cased my own jobs . . . Then . . ."

"Then you got greedy?"

"Then I became a humanist. Mr. Nice Guy." He coughed bitter laughter out of his throat like phlegm. "Jamie Cardwell, an old Army buddy from Nam, came to me because he was into a Shylock for a lot of dough. Degenerate gambler, on partial disability from Nam, married, kid coming . . ."

"And he had this perfect setup?" she prompted.

"You've heard my stories before, too," he said. "Jamie could get the combination to a wholesale jeweler's safe, he could get me into the building and back out again—"

151

"Moyers told me a guard saw you getting away and shot you."

"Did he tell you the guard was named Jamie Cardwell?"

Betrayal opened before her like curtains on a play. "My God!" she breathed, stunned.

"It seems Jamie'd taken in a couple of partners he forgot to mention—the Shylock and the jeweler's son. But the double-cross was all his. He was afraid there wasn't going to be enough money to get him out of the hole." He snorted in bitter amusement. "All he had to do was ask—I'd have given him my share. I was in it for him in the first place."

Louise said hesitantly, "The man who was killed in the penthouse. Tenconi. Was he the Shylock who—"

"Yeah. Shot to death four hours after I kicked him in the balls and met the maid as I walked out. I don't know who killed him, but his partner stepped into his percentage."

"That's who you came down here to avoid," she said.

"And that's why I need Moyers on my tail—as a witness to the fact that I'm not involved if there's any more killing."

"Hey, big fella," she said, "you've got a witness right here, you know."

"The cops'll believe it better coming from him."

They were silent for long moments, staring out over the darkening valley. Louise realized his expression had become difficult to read in the gathering dusk. When she finally spoke it was almost reluctantly, as if she were afraid of shattering the mood.

"Why don't you just . . . give them the diamonds? I know they cost you eight years, but you said yourself you'd have given your share to Cardwell if he'd asked. You could walk away clean . . ."

Runyan stood up. "We'd better get started. It's just a walk down the backside of the mountain, but guys keep getting killed. They miss their step in the dark and fall a thousand feet into the river. They never even get a chance to drown."

Bleary outrage welled up like trapped stomach gas. Cardwell slid over to the edge of the booth to stand up, ruining the moment by getting poked in the groin by the corner of the table. He looked down at Delarty's indifferent face.

"Leave me out of it," he said. "Just leave me out of it."

"You were never fucking in it, Cardwell," said Delarty.

A pair of dimes plonged in the slot of the outdoor pay phone across Judah from *Killeen's*. As Cardwell came out of the bar hunched down in his belligerently working-class windbreaker, a seven-digit number was tapped out.

"Police emergency, operator six," said the flat depersonalized voice of the police dispatcher. Every few seconds the call was beeped to show it was being recorded.

"Cardwell is the name," said the caller in a near-whisper. "Cardwell. C-a-r-d-w-e-l-l. You got that?"

Cardwell was walking out Judah toward his house several blocks away on the parallel street, Kirkham.

"Cardwell," repeated the dispatcher's phone-filtered voice. "Yes, I have that. What's the . . ."

"Ask Runyan about it," the man whispered. "R-u-n-y-a-n. Just out of the joint for a week or so. Ask him about Tenconi, too. T-e-n-c-o-n-i. The maid saw him leaving."

He hung up before the dispatcher could ask any more questions. The door squealed when he left the booth.

Runyan and Louise walked side by side through the almost warm valley evening, past other strollers. Though it was only a little after seven, she could barely keep her eyes open.

"More lies," she said abruptly.

"Yours or mine?"

She kept her eyes straight ahead and said in a rush of words, "I didn't come back on my own. *He* asked me to and I said I would and then I—"

"I know. I heard your phone calls. In Tiburon. Here, last night—"

Louise felt a bursting rush of emotion as the long-suppressed lump of guilt was hurled through the last barrier in her mind like a stone through a window pane. She wanted to laugh, cry, sing, dance, get drunk, kick a slipper full of champagne off an archbishop's head.

"I'm glad Cardwell didn't kill you either time," she said. "I'm getting rather fond of you."

"It's a strange feeling to realize that the guy whose guts you've hated for eight years is just a shell—scared, shaky, a real boozer, a real loser . . . If there's anything worse than being a con, I guess it's being Jamie Cardwell."

Cardwell trudged stolidly up the terrazzo front steps to his inset front door and started to find the lock with his key, his hand not as rock-steady as it might have been. Betty'd have plenty to say about that, but what was a guy supposed to do? At least he'd told off that bastard Delarty. Delarty, Runyan, all of them—they'd learn that if you tried to play pussy with Jamie Cardwell, you were gonna get . . .

The silenced muzzle of a .38 revolver was pressed against his left temple. He could smell the Hoppe's No. 9 that had been used to clean it. He didn't even raise his hands, just rolled doleful eyes toward the dull glint of streetlight off the unseen killer's weapon. His whole life didn't pass before his eyes; he felt only an overwhelming sadness.

"Aw hell," he said in a tired voice, "I just *knew* I was never going to get out of this al—"

The gun jerked and puffed as it had through the peephole in Tenconi's penthouse door, driving Cardwell's head sideways against the door frame like a grotesque fist. He slid down the painted wood, leaving a wet wavering snail-track of blood and brain behind.

Runyan had taken a small plastic pill bottle from his pocket; he kept tossing it into the air and catching it again as they strolled. They were almost back to Camp Four. Louise gave an involuntary jaw-creaking yawn.

"What are you going to do about them, Runyan? They expect their cut and you don't have anything to give them."

"I'm going to duck out on Moyers and steal some stolen bearer bonds off another thief down in Los Angeles."

"So all this rock climbing wasn't just fun and games," she said almost accusingly. "It was brushing up on old skills."

He nuzzled her neck. "I like you 'cause you're smart and you smell good."

Louise drew away from him, a frosty glint in her eye.

"And when did you plan to pull this little caper?"

"Tonight."

"*Tonight?*" She said in ominous tones, "What was supposed to happen to me while you were off having all your fun?"

Runyan flipped the plastic pill bottle in her direction. She caught it adroitly, then stopped in the middle of the road to read the label aloud in the dim light.

"Restoril, fifteen milligrams. Take two caps before bedtime." She looked at him and exclaimed, "Sleeping pills!"

She hurled the bottle at him. He caught it and, with the same movement, tossed it into the roadside ditch.

He started walking again. Louise ran after him. She bumped him hard with her hip, then put an arm around his waist and rested her head on his shoulder.

"Kid," she said, "I like your moves."

Runyan started to laugh.

Louise was at the top of a mountain in a medieval walled city. The sun was very bright; in every direction there were jagged mountains to and from which people were flying with the aid of equipment on their backs that looked like scuba gear. The people had come, she knew, for that gear which let them fly.

She had also come for power, but not to fly. She had to

speak to the General in charge—she needed his help in a decision which she had to stick to, she knew, or die.

The General was standing in the middle of the main square, very tall, unmilitary even though wearing a dark uniform. She pushed through the crowd of petitioners and asked him to help her. He shook his head.

"Not now. There's a plague in the city, and I have too much to do. Not now."

To detain him, Louise reached over and seized the General's penis with her hand. It did not seem a strange thing to do, nor did it seem odd that his member was bare despite the uniform he wore. She came awake in a panic, working her hand up and down the quickly stiffening cock, sure Runyan had given her the sleeping pills and was about to sneak away without her.

Instead, he was rolling over on top of her, still half-asleep himself. She quickly opened her legs, with a gasp of mingled pleasure and relief felt his thick shaft pushing into her. His strokes were long and slow, steady as a heartbeat; when they rose to orgasm she arched her head against the ground so hard that her neck creaked, and raked his back with clawed fingers. He licked her eyelids, licked the corners of her mouth, kissed her on the chin before regretfully withdrawing his still half-rigid member.

Louise sat up, yawning, sated, fumbling in the dim light of the torch for the bra and panties abandoned for her quick dive into the sleeping bag three hours before. Only then did she remember the question which had been bothering her when she had gone to sleep.

"If using our car would alert Moyers to the fact that we're leaving, how are we going to get to the airfield in time?"

"We're going to steal one of the Park Service jeeps. Hell, what are thieves for?"

It was just 10:30 when Runyan turned off California 140 in the rolling grassy hills a few miles southwest of the park entrance at El Portal. He followed a narrow rutted dirt track that bounced and tossed the stolen jeep about like an Australian surfboat coming in through the breakers. One instant their headlights were glinting off the scrub oaks, the next casting long shadows behind a lichen-covered boulder, then making twin glowing rubies of the eyes of a startled mule deer.

Going across the flat grassy surface of the airfield, their lights picked out the night-deserted quonset-hut hangar and office with the airsock hanging limp from the mast on the roof.

"I always wondered what it was like to be a rodeo rider," Louise yelled above the noise of the jeep.

She heard a plane's engines turn over, cough, catch. It smoothed out and a trim white plane with a blue decorative stripe running along the side began trundling slowly forward from among a half-dozen others tied down. Runyan stopped the jeep.

"Taps Turner knows how to do things in style," he said. "Twin-motor Aztec-C. We'll be to Burbank in two hours."

The black woman pilot in a red jumpsuit, huge black radio earphones making her head resemble that of a gigantic fly, didn't even unstrap while they boarded. Instead, she demanded, "Who the fuck is this?"

Runyan tossed the carefully packed black nylon stuff bag into the back of the cabin, then stood on the wing to help Louise into her seat. "My mother. She wanted to see the cherry blossoms in bloom."

His eyes were challenging, glinting with either excitement or anger. After a long moment, the pilot sighed and turned away toward the instrument panel. "Sheee-it, mother," she said, giving the first word two syllables, "ain't no cherries in L.A.—let alone blossoms. Just mah-ture fruits with grey chest hair and medallions on gold chains."

The plane was moving even as Runyan climbed into the

copilot's seat; it bumped and jittered as it gained speed, as if it were a handy target for anger that should have been directed at Runyan. The landing lights tossed exaggerated shadows out beyond the clumps and tufts of grass on the runway. They slanted up and away sharply, the engine almost stalling.

She picked up California 99 and followed it down the fertile San Joaquin Valley, the land just blackness below them, pinpointed with farm lights and the moving broken firefly chains of traffic on the highway. The I-5 Grapevine showed the way through the San Gabriel Mountains, which cup Los Angeles down to the sea, giving it both its climate and its smog. After locking on to the Burbank radio beam, she jerked off her big earphones to glare at him.

"Louise," he said, "I'd like you to meet Grace."

Grace was a stunningly beautiful woman, Louise realized, five or six years younger than she. And not at all interested in Louise. She spurned the proffered hand.

"I thought you was a fucking professional," she said to Runyan.

He sang loudly, "I'm a beauty, I'm a daisy, I'm humpbacked, I'm crazy, I'm knock-kneed and bow-legged as well!" He grinned. "A song my daddy taught me." He grabbed the controls and jerked the half-wheel over and down to the left.

"Whut're your doin', honky shit toad?" shrieked Grace.

It was instantly apparent that Runyan knew exactly what he was doing. As she tried unsuccessfully to wrest back control of the plane from him, he executed a rapid series of intricate maneuvers—Immelmanns, barrel rolls, stalls. Then he levelled her off and picked up the Burbank radio beam again.

"It's just like riding a bike, Grace," he said. "You never forget how."

"I knew you were fucking trouble the moment you walked into Taps's office," she muttered.

"Was thrown in," Runyan corrected her. "This isn't trouble, Grace. This is the end of trouble."

CHAPTER 25

It was 1:21 in the morning. As they passed the Sunset Boulevard exit, Grace got the rented Cougar into the right lane of the San Diego Freeway. Traffic was late-night fast but light. Louise was beside her in the front seat; Taps and Runyan were in the back. The night was clear and dark and crisp, 20 degrees warmer than Yosemite had been.

"Brother Blood's out making a coke buy," said Taps. "You got one hour for sure, maybe more."

"An hour's enough," said Runyan, fighting to keep the irritation out of his voice. Pregame tension.

"So you keep telling me," said Taps. Tension strummed in his voice also.

They must have gone over the plan in broad strokes a hundred, two hundred times in Q, a fantasy scheme to pass a few of the endless prison hours. Now it was happening.

Grace took the Wilshire Boulevard exit, following the off-ramp down and around under the freeway past the sterile landscaped Veterans Administration, then east on Wilshire past the anachronistic one-story red-roofed Ships Restaurant in Westwood, a gaudy soft palate for the new high-rise condo teeth that lined Wilshire like multimillion-dollar inlays. A half mile beyond, she turned off near the ultraprivate L.A. Country Club.

She turned again, then slowed to crawl past a pair of high-rise condos that took up an entire block. She pointed.

"Brother Blood's penthouse is in the one on the right."

"You go in the one on the left," said Taps unnecessarily. "Not so much security."

Runyan didn't say anything at all. He wished Taps hadn't come up with that idea about Runyan not leaving the penthouse with the bonds on his person. He desperately wanted it not to mean the obvious, but he'd have to find out the hard way.

Grace turned right at the next corner, then right again and stopped. They were now behind the buildings. Runyan took a deep silent breath, gripped his black nylon stuff bag.

"Twelve minutes," he told the back of Grace's head as he opened his door and stepped out into the street.

Without turning, she said, "I'll be ready."

Runyan closed his door without slamming, went around behind the back of the waiting car to the curb side. Although the street was residential-area deserted, he could hear occasional cars on Wilshire two blocks away. Louise reached a hand out of her window and he took it. Her skin was warm, almost hot, as if she were slightly feverish.

"Eight years," he said with a nervous grin. Eight years in the belly of the beast.

"Eight years better," Louise said.

Runyan nodded jauntily; his jitters had disappeared at her words. Taps stuck his head and one arm out of the rear window; the manicured nail of his long brown forefinger made tiny ticking noises against the crystal of his watch.

"The power goes off fifteen minutes after Grace goes in. Then you got ninety seconds to get on and off the cable, or—"

"Or I fry," said Runyan.

"And remember Brother Blood owns the damn building, so when you've made the switch—"

"I know what to do," Runyan said flatly.

Grace drove aimlessly to kill the extra minutes. Taps leaned his forearms on the back of the front seat, his head behind and between those of the two women in front of him.

"We got a couple minutes for insurance. Swing by the dealer's an' make sure Brother Blood is where he's spozed to be."

They crossed Beverly Glen on Lindbrook, near Holmby drove by a long black Mercedes limo with a middle-aged black chauffeur leaning against the front fender and smoking a fat brown cigar.

"Yeah!" exclaimed Taps. "We're on!"

Grace drove the Cougar back the way she had come, stopped on a side street a block from the condos. Taps got out; he wore work clothes and a Dodgers souvenir baseball cap and carried an electrician's tool box.

"You got five minutes," he warned Grace.

"I be late, shugah," she drawled, "you fire my ass."

Taps watched the car drive away. It was all expensive homes here, in the multi-hundred-thousand-dollar range. Pool man on Mondays, wetback Mexican gardeners on Wednesdays, private school for the kids, vacation in Puerto Vallarta with Europe every third year. Well, his turn now.

He walked quickly back to a manhole cover flush with the concrete, took a stubby wrecking bar out from under his windbreaker, inserted the bent end into the socket, and heaved the cover aside. It grated loudly in the still night air. He sat down on the edge, found the ladder with his toes, shot another look around, then went down out of sight. The cover grated back, clanging dully into place. The street was deserted again.

Grace had parked the Cougar in mid-block so it wasn't really in front of either high-rise. Louise, leaning back against the locked door on her side of the car, watched Grace use the tipped-down rear-view mirror to make herself into a whore. Grace caught her eye in the mirror and winked.

"Your man's gonna be just fine, honey," she said.

"I thought you didn't like him," said Louise coldly. "Said he was trouble."

From a handbag big enough to hold an Uzi machine gun, she took purple three-inch spikes and a bright purple silk scarf. She cinched the scarf tight around her middle, leaving the ends hanging over one hip. Then she jerked the zipper of her shimmery red jumpsuit down almost to her navel.

"I like you and him together, shugah," she drawled. "You go by your gut feelin' with a man, you don't never be wrong."

She wore no brassiere; her breasts were magnificent, bared almost to the edge of the areolas, but she frowned down at them, then began rolling her nipples between her fingers and thumbs until they stood up boldly against the thin satin material.

Finally she looked over at Louise. "How do I look?"

"Like a two-dollar quickie on the back seat."

Grace winked again. "You got it, shugah."

She opened her door and got out. Louise slid over under the wheel. She had always considered herself quite sophisticated; Grace made her feel young and naive as a virgin.

She called, "Good luck." Grace turned and gave her a street-urchin's grin and a thumbs-up signal, then cut at an angle across the carefully barbered and lit lawn toward the front entrance of the condo which did not have Brother Blood's penthouse perched on top of it.

Picking any lock takes a certain amount of time and a great deal of skill. It is not the simple matter that television would have us believe. Nobody ever picked a lock with one pick; at the outset a tension tool—an L-shaped piece of spring steel—

must be inserted into the keyhole and turned slightly so that as each pin is raised to its shear line the tension will keep it from falling back down into the core.

Runyan had spent 2.5 minutes trying to "rake" the lock of the basement rear service entrance of the high-rise—the quick and easy way which sometimes works in a matter of seconds—then had gotten serious: another 7.55 minutes with his tension tool and a curved-tip pick before the lock finally yielded.

He made no move to open the door, instead held it just fractionally ajar; he knew that a closed-circuit TV scanning camera was covering the inside of it. The luminous dial of his watch told him there was less than a minute to go.

Emery Samnic was 47 years old, had been married to the same woman for 26 years and despite this—or because of it—had his sexual fantasies like any other man. For five nights a week he wore the uniform of a security guard and sat behind the security desk in the high-rise lobby.

It was good duty. Tipped back in his swivel chair, he had only to turn his head to examine the bank of TV screen monitors set against the back of the security cubicle. The monitors covered the condo's entrances, doorways, corridors, and the interiors of the elevators. In one a guard walked a corridor; the others showed nothing at all.

Then a beautiful black woman appeared in the front entrance monitor to push the night buzzer. It sounded behind Emery's desk. She waited with a hip thrust out provocatively, her big gaudy handbag tucked under one arm, tapping a three-inch spike against the pavement, a thin brown cigar between her lips.

There was no one else with her, but Emery stood up and loosened the Smith and Wesson .38 Police Special in his belt holster before pushing the button to release the door catch.

On the screen, the black woman opened the door and disappeared. The real Grace, in living color, simultaneously came across the lobby toward his desk, her heels clop-clopping on the terrazzo, everything moving the way women's bodies moved in his fantasies. Her expression was go-to-hell and she obviously wore no bra or panties under the clinging red jumpsuit.

Emery cleared his throat and said, "This isn't your sort of place, sister."

Grace put her elbows on his counter, thrusting out her butt and languidly blowing smoke in his face.

"I is *invited*, honey." She had a slightly husky voice.

She could see past Emery's thick waist to the basement monitor. Runyan opened the loading door and entered boldly. She leaned closer yet, giving Emery the news all the way to her navel. As Runyan walked over to the freight elevator and pushed the button, Grace pointed at the house phone with a very long synthetic purple nail.

"Why don't you phone up the man and find out? Apartment . . . Two-Three-Seven."

What sort of business would the Rotzels have with this sort of woman at almost two in the morning? The old man was a deacon of the Baptist church, for Pete sake.

"This time of night . . ." he began, letting it hang.

Grace moved her cleavage closer; across the lobby, the elevator indicator glowed as the cage descended to Runyan.

"It was a *urgent* phone call, shugah," she said. "I swear I think that man was watching a dirty movie and he's got his *motor* running, you know what I mean . . ."

Emery knew what she meant: He could feel his dork pushing out against the heavy twill uniform pants. Jesus, what would it be like to put the old banana into something like that?

He unconsciously blew out a deep breath and picked up the house phone and tapped out two-three-seven. On the monitors, the elevator door opened and Runyan stepped through, disappearing from the basement screen to be instantly picked up by the adjacent elevator camera. Grace could hear an angry squawking voice on the phone. Hurry, Runyan, damn you!

Emery said unhappily into the phone, "This is Emery on the lobby desk downstairs. I'm sorry to disturb you, sir, but there's a young lady here who says . . ." He broke off to listen to more squawks, finally said, "I know what time it is, sir, I surely do, but she says you wanted . . ."

Grace, watching Runyan spring up and knock open the elevator ceiling trap, reached across the counter to grab the phone out of Emery's hand.

"Lemme talk to him," she said, then said into the phone, "Listen, buster, you phone up an' say you needs an Around the World, *bad*, now what's this shit about—"

"Who *is* this?" demanded a high scratchy man's voice. "How *dare* you use language like that to me? My wife and I are Christian people who—"

"So you got your old lady there, so I takes care of her too," said Grace, winking at the open-mouthed Emery. "All it'll cost you is an extra fifty—"

"I'm going to call the police and report you!" shrieked the man on the phone. On the monitor, Runyan was tossing his stuff bag up through the ceiling trap. In front of her, Emery was starting to turn toward the monitors. Grace quickly thrust the phone back into his hands.

"Man wanta talk to you."

On the monitor, Runyan crouched for his leap.

On the phone, the confused Emery said, "I . . . I'm real sorry, Mr. Rotzel, I didn't know she was going to—"

"*Rotzel?*"

Grace reached over and broke the connection in mid-word. Behind Emery, Runyan leaped up and grabbed the edges of the trap.

"Rotzel ain't the name of the dude phone up! What's this here address?"

"Uh . . . Twelve-Forty-two Boningto—"

"*Shee*-it, shugah, I got the wrong building!"

Grace winked at Emery and swivelled her way toward the door, her exaggerated hip swing holding his lusting eyes long enough for Runyan to disappear through the trap in the elevator ceiling. As the door closed behind Grace, Emery wiped the sheen of sweat from his forehead and whirled belatedly to check the monitors. Everything was serene, nothing moving anywhere.

CHAPTER 26

Standing on the roof of the elevator cage, Runyan fit the Jumars to the cable. The clock was really running now. He put his feet in the slings and, black nylon stuff bag clipped to his belt, began walking himself up the cable. Could it have been just two days ago that Louise had watched him do this under the overhang on Monday Morning Slab?

Under the street two blocks away, Taps Turner was moving cautiously along one of the utility access tunnels by the light of a tiny powerful halogen-bulb flashlight. He set down his electrician's kit in front of a switch box bolted to one wall and used his prybar to break the padlock hasp. Inside the hinged cover were rows of engaged knife switches. He began to compare the interior layout of the box with a wiring diagram, humming a Lionel Ritchie love ballad softly under his breath.

Louise drove the Cougar while Grace wiped the makeup off

her face with a wad of kleenex. They both were laughing at her tale of Emery's wandering eyes and bulging pants.

In the elevator shaft, Runyan grunted his way upward. The air was close and smelled of hot metal and lubricating oil. The day on Royal Arches had taken a lot out of him, but it had insured his physical confidence, made it possible for him to be here now. His movements were crisp, without hesitation, exact. He had no "protection" in place—he was working without a safety line—so the strength of his grip on the Jumars and the sureness of his feet in the slings were his only insurance against falling as he practiced this mild form of . . . what? Masochism? Maybe self-abuse. His body was sure feeling abused as he climbed the cable.

Endlessly.

He rested a moment, panting, tipped his head back to look up into the dimness of the shaft. The big cable wheels still seemed a long way up.

He went into the fugue state he had perfected while practicing gymnastics at Q, trying to pass the endless hours of confinement. One of the prison survival skills you never heard about was infinite patience. He had learned it.

What was Louise doing right now? He checked his watch. Still driving around; she wouldn't park the car near the other condo's underground garage entrance until about five minutes before he was scheduled to be coming out.

He shoved up a Jumar, and it rapped against the rim of the grooved wheel over which the cable passed.

He'd made it!

Runyan grabbed the nearest spoke of the wheel, made sure of his grip, then carefully disengaged his feet from the Jumar slings to swing his legs up and hook them around the wheel rim.

Hanging backward under it like a sloth under a branch, he removed the Jumars from the cable with his free hand and clipped them to carabiners threaded on his belt. From there it was a cinch to climb the spokes of the massive wheel and step onto the metal gridwork service platform.

The housing door, as on the diagram he had studied, opened out onto the blacktopped roof of the building. He stopped for a few moments, massaging the tautness from his arms while gulping fresh night air. Still on time. He negotiated the mini obstacle course of capped chimneys and vents to the edge of the building that faced the twin high-rise a hundred feet away. On the inside of the four-foot-high concrete parapet a sign held to the wall with cement screws read: DANGER—HIGH TENSION.

He bent across the top of the low wall to look down. Bingo. A very thick black power cable ran along the outside of the building five feet below, did a right angle through a terminal box, and stretched away into the darkness toward Brother Blood's building. Right where it was supposed to be.

Runyan checked his watch again, unclipped the stuff bag from his belt, set it on the roof, and took out a break-'em-shake-'em, cracked and twisted and shook the short rod until it glowed with a soft cool green light like Darth Vader's sword. He bent it into a horseshoe around his neck. Break-'em-shake-'ems left the hands free, a vital factor in rock climbing.

He zipped the bag, clipped it back on the belt, unclipped his Jumars, and put them on the top of the parapet. Then he jumped up so he was sitting between them, facing in. One minute before two a.m. He edged himself back across the top of the wall until his butt was hanging off into space. This was the tricky part. He now was supported only by his hands gripping the outside angle of the top and the outer wall and by his heels hooked over the inside edge of the wall.

Runyan hyperventilated, focusing his energies to that white-hot physical point that perhaps only athletes know, then let his knees slowly bend, arching his body slowly back and down. Now only his heels hooked over that inner edge, and his calves along the top of the wall, supported his body;

he was hanging face-out, upside down above the high tension cable terminal.

He groped above him on top of the parapet for one of the Jumars, found it, brought it slowly down in front of his face. If he should drop it now, everything was over.

In the tunnel, Tap's glowing watch digits read 1:59:58 and :59 and 2:00:00 and his hands, in place on two of the knife switches, pulled them down to disengage them.

In the Cougar, Louise was just turning into the block where the high-rises were when all the lights went out except the street lights. She grabbed Grace's arm in her excitement.

"It's happenin', baby, it's happenin'!" responded Grace in a voice almost guttural with tension.

Hanging upside down by the green glow of his break-'em-shake-'em, supported by his calves and heels on the parapet, Runyan jammed the first Jumar into place, squeezing it down so the brake bit into the high-tension core of the cable with its relentless grip. If the power had not been cut, he would just be smoking meat.

He found the second Jumar, fixed it into place. The seconds ticked away in his head. Only 90 of them before Taps re-engaged the knife switches.

Gripping the Jumars with iron hands, he kicked off the building. His body swung out and down and around, his arms and hands taking the full shocking jolt of his weight as he jerked up under the cable. He was now hanging from the Jumars only by his grip, which already had loosened the brakes so he was sliding down the cable toward Brother Blood's building.

Emery skittered his flashlight beam around a lobby lit only by the streetlights outside. Over by the elevators a second guard's flash danced and probed.

"It isn't just us, Emery," he called.

Emery felt a great weight lift off him. He had been afraid it might somehow have something to do with that black hooker who had showed up. "Okay, then, I'll call Water and Power," he said.

Runyan, still lit only by his break-'em-shake-'em, walked the Jumars quickly up the cable toward the junction box on Brother Blood's building, panting with nonstop effort as the seconds exploded in his brain. At the box he reached over, a hand at a time, to grab the bare power cable. Then he kipped himself up into a full pressout. He got a foot up onto the cable, a knee, was balancing on the wire, grabbed the edge of the parapet and jerked his feet up off the cable.

There were crackling bursts of white light as the Jumars, scorched and smoking, fell away. The lights flickered on in the buildings as he muscled himself up onto the wall and dropped over onto the roof.

He ran lightly across a patio landscaped with expensive potted greenery and shrubs to the sliding glass doors of the penthouse. It looked like a lock that might be reasonable about raking. Since the penthouse was supposedly the only way to the roof, he didn't have to worry about alarms.

Louise had pulled over to the curb and stopped when the lights had gone out. Now, 90 seconds later, they were back on again. She whirled on Grace.

"Did he make it? *Did he*?"

"I didn't see no falling bodies," smiled Grace. "Relax, shugah. That man of yours, he's a survivor." She dug an elbow into Louise's ribs. "Let's get moving again, baby. Don't wanta draw no po-leece before Taps can get out of that manhole."

With a thrust of his powerful shoulders, Taps heaved the manhole cover aside. He grabbed the tool kit from where it was wedged between him and the ladder, set it on the street, then leaped nimbly up on the pavement himself. He kicked the manhole cover, clanging, back into place before running to the sidewalk.

He had taken only half a dozen jaunty and unconcerned steps when a power company truck came rumbling around the corner and stopped beside the manhole. The uniformed workmen who got out never even glanced his way.

Runyan slid open one of the glass doors, entered, shut and locked it carefully behind him, then pushed his way through the drapes into the spacious living room. It was sumptuous and decorator perfect in the dim glow of his break-'em-shake-'em.

The study also was a decorator's wet dream: thick carpets, microcomputer and letter-quality printer, massive hardwood desk, overstuffed leather executive's swivel chair that looked ready to fly, waist-to-ceiling bookshelves behind the desk, silver-edged trophy plaques on the walls.

"Coke-Dealer-of-the-Year Award," muttered Runyan. He shut the door and returned his break-'em-shake-'em to the stuff bag after turning on the lights. His time was almost up.

The telephone was a futuristic model with memory; on one side of it was a black oblong box with six buttons on it, on the other a computer modem cradle for the receiver. The phone was the key to the safe, but here Taps's intelligence was vague. Runyan pushed the top button on the black box. The stereo deck started to play. He pushed it again. The stereo stopped.

Second button. The maple doors slid open on the huge console TV and the set switched on. Again. Off.

Third. Lights on and off.

Fourth. Window blinds.

When Runyan pushed the fifth button, a panel of the book-shelves, books and all, swung open to reveal a small wall safe of hardened cadmium steel. Runyan tried the swing handle.

Locked. Since there was no visible dial, the box with the buttons on it probably also opened the door of the safe.

He went back to the desk and pushed the final button. Nothing happened. Again. The safe was still locked.

But it had to have something to do with the box and its buttons. How would the mind of a Brother Blood work? Intricate mind. Liked games. Liked gadgets. A sly and tricky dude . . .

And a dude who played around with a computer. A computer which had a modem for communicating with other computers through the telephone. What if this modem had a different function? He picked up the phone receiver and fitted it into the computer modem. Then he punched the final button again. Nothing.

One last thing to try. He flicked on the black rocker switch on the back of the computer. Tried again. The door of the safe popped open an inch.

Yeah. The games people play. Here's to you, Brother Blood. He switched off the computer and took from the stuff bag the stacks of ornately-scrolled counterfeit bearer bonds which had been forged to Grace's order. Inside the safe were exactly similar stacks of genuine bearer bonds with the same sequenced serial numbers. He put these stacks on the far end of the desk. It would be disastrous to mix them up.

Taps cut off from the sidewalk between bushes to the rear wall of Brother Blood's building. He had just put down his electrician's box when a thin nylon cord set down Runyan's black nylon stuff bag a dozen feet away. Taps slashed the cord with his switchblade and walked away with the bag, not glancing back, not bothering with his tool kit.

At the corner was an open pay phone without a booth. He looked quickly, almost guiltily around, then slotted his dimes and tapped out a seven-digit local number.

"Yeah," he said into the phone. "I want to talk with Brother Blood. Tell him Taps Turner is calling."

CHAPTER 27

When Louise turned the corner, she saw Taps talking and gesturing earnestly on the pay phone. Beside her, Grace drew in a sharp breath.

"That rotten son of a bitch! Stop the car!"

She was out before it stopped moving, leaving her door hanging open and Louise gaping after her, open-mouthed, as she ran across the grass strip toward the phone where Taps was just saying "Okay, that be cool . . ."

Grace snatched the receiver out of hand and slammed it back onto the hooks. He backhanded her across the face, yelping in astonishment, "You *crazy*, woman? Wuffo you—"

Grace was yelling, "*He saved your life! You owe him!*"

He grabbed her by the arms and started shaking her, barely aware of Louise's pale shocked face framed in the open car door a few yards away.

"*We got the bonds, all of 'em!*" Seeing some of the wildness fading from Grace's eyes, he gingerly released his grip on her

176

arms. In a quieter voice, he said, "Wasn't no way we could do that except make sure he couldn't ever come back at us."

"You did it 'cause he saved your ass in prison," said Grace in a low, intense voice. "There ain't a livin' soul in this world you'd do that for, an' you can't stand thinkin' about it." She gave a harsh laugh. "And now Brother Blood's gonna take you down, nigger."

Taps hesitated when, in the background, their car suddenly fishtailed away, so abruptly that Grace's open door slammed shut. He felt sudden fear. Grace wasn't hardly ever wrong, and now the white bitch Runyan had brought along had cut out with their car, stranding them. But he said, "You . . . You're crazy, woman."

"Don't you see it yet?" she asked in an almost tired voice. "Brother Blood, he's gonna start wonderin', How that man know to call me at the dealer's unless he was in on it an' just chicken' out at the last minute?" Over his protestations, she continued, "It's what you'd think, was you. Ain't Brother Blood gonna be any different." She shook her head and turned away from him. "I ain't hangin' around to die with no boot dumb as you."

Taps let her get almost to the sidewalk before he called after her, "But I got the bonds, baby!"

She turned to look at him, almost with pity. "You got shit, Taps. You think Runyan didn't know you planned to cross him when you asked he th'ow those bonds down to you?"

She trudged away, her steps tapping out a jaunty staccato in marked contrast to the slump of her shoulders. Taps wanted to run after her, grab her, make it right. But he had to know about this first. He ripped open the black stuff bag with his switchblade in a frenzy of anticipation and dread. It was full of newspapers folded to the approximate size of bearer bonds.

Runyan stepped into Brother Blood's private elevator and pushed the GARAGE button next to the LOBBY and PENT-

HOUSE buttons. Tight security. He touched the bulky oblong under his sweater. If Taps was waiting for him across the street from the garage entrance, then everything was straight; if not, yet another friend had betrayed him. He was running out of people who hadn't tried it, one way or another. Even Louise . . .

Ashcan that. It was all in the past. They were together now for the long run.

Taps Turner had a terminal case of the stupids, thought Brother Blood. Planning to steal the bond stash—with a white dude, yet!—and then chickening out and thinking he'd be dumb enough to swallow the con about stumbling across the robbery! No, Taps was dog meat right now, he just didn't know it yet.

Brother Blood was a tall lean bald hollow-eyed man, impeccably dressed in a three-piece midnight blue suit and mirror-shined black oxfords. He leaned forward to peer out of the windshield past the beefy shoulder of his bodyguard as the stretch limo whispered down the deserted street beside his apartment building.

They turned the corner. The driver pushed the remote electronic-eye activator. Fifty yards away, the heavy steel mesh gate began rattling upward. As it did, a lean dark-haired white man in black slacks and black sweater emerged from the garage, walking quickly. His hands were empty, but Brother Blood's practiced, suspicious eye could pick out the ex-con.

"That's him," he said to his driver. "Run him down."

Much too late, Runyan heard the almost silent rush of the limo coming at him. Even as he hurled himself desperately to the side, he knew he would be dead before he hit the concrete.

That was when Louise, seat-belted in and with the accelerator floored, rammed Grace's car into the rear fender of the limo. The impact knocked it sideways just enough so its nose missed Runyan by the necessary fraction as he landed, tucked, rolled, and came up running.

Not away. At. He was aware with an edge of his consciousness that Louise's car, slewed around by the impact, had spun broadside into a power pole on the other side of the still-deserted street. No fire, no explosion, and she was trying to open her sprung door: probably unhurt. She had not only saved his life; she had bought him just enough time.

Since the windshield was bullet-proof glass, the bodyguard, a thick-set black gorilla with wary eyes, already had his door open and his head and arm stuck out to fire at Runyan. But Runyan was high in the air; a piston-drive snap of both legs kicked the door shut again.

The bodyguard slumped down halfway out of the car, his skull creased on one side by the edge of the door, on the other by the edge of the frame. Brother Blood, partway out of the back seat, looked up into the black eye of his bodyguard's gun in Runyan's hand. He threw his arms up and wide; Brother Blood was a survivor too. Runyan gestured him away from the car and up against the wall of his building with movements of the heavy-caliber automatic.

"I won't forget this," he said in a soft deadly voice.

"Don't," said Runyan. He swung the gun toward the chauffeur, who was trying to fit himself under the dash like a stereo.

"I . . . I just drive, sir," the chauffeur said quickly.

Runyan gestured again. "Not any more. Not tonight."

The chauffeur opened the door on his side and scuttled out on his hands and knees, then came erect and backed away into the center of the street, arms high, face gleaming with an earnest sweat of nonviolent intentions.

Louise had managed to kick open her car door. She ran across the street to the limo. She slid in under the steering wheel. Runyan heaved the unconscious bodyguard out of the way so he could get in beside her.

"I think we probably should leave," he said.

Louise rammed it into reverse and gunned it backwards, bouncing off the curb into the street. The back wheel rubbed on the fender, but would turn. Runyan slammed his door as she put it into drive and shot ahead down the street. He tossed the guard's .45 out into the gutter through the still-hanging-open back door, then slammed that, too.

"Thanks, darling, is sort of inadequate," he said.

"All part of the service." Laughter danced in her eyes; she was having the time of her life. "Burbank airport?"

"You got it."

Louise suddenly sobered. "What are we going to do, baby? You're as bad off as you were before. Taps has the bonds and you still have to find the cash somewhere to—"

"*We* have the bonds," Runyan corrected her. He pulled up his sweater and took out the wad of securities. "I figured Taps for a double cross, so I kept them just in case." He laughed. "I've learned *something* in the last eight years."

It was well after dark when Louise drove across the Bay Bridge into San Francisco. They had left Grace's plane at the little country airfield, returned the Park Service jeep to the chain link fence behind the maintenance shed, and slept into the early afternoon before breaking camp and packing up their gear. On the way up, Runyan was delighted to catch a glimpse of Moyers's car behind them on the freeway.

"This is the next tricky part," he told her as they took the first skyway off-ramp after the bridge. "We have to stash the bonds without Moyers knowing anything about them. I think it'll work because he's relying on that beeper he planted on our car. Turn here."

Louise swung the Toyota into First Street from Mission. It was an area of sandwich shops, a coin arcade, wholesale office furniture dealers. To their left crouched the dark mass of the Trans-Bay Terminal; it also housed the Trailways Bus Depot.

"Slow around the block twice," said Runyan. "The second time, use the alley."

He jumped out of the moving car, cut behind it ducking other vehicles, took a long running leap to the sidewalk. Before the startled Louise even lost sight of him in her rearview mirror, he was into the terminal.

Hidden from the street but able to see cars after they had passed, he waited just inside the door. Thirty seconds later, Moyers drove by. Runyan grinned to himself and turned away.

He crossed the nearly empty, echoing, low-roofed waiting room, past the lighted ticket windows to the bank of coin lockers flanking the Fremont Street entrance, chose one in which to stuff the thick sheaf of securities from under his sweater. Key in hand, he walked over to one of the phone booths and entered it.

Louise had gone out First Street to Folsom, turned left, at Fremont had turned left again. She kept checking the rearview mirror, but she saw no sign of Moyers. Was he back there? Or had he guessed Runyan's strategy and stopped by the terminal to check out the waiting room?

She waited for a rattling almost-empty electric trolley to leave the terminal, then turned into Mission, at First turned again to start her second round. A motorcyclist paced her for half a block, ogling her and darting his tongue in and out between bearded lips.

What if Runyan wasn't . . .

He would be there, dammit.

She turned into Howard instead of going down to Mission again. Buses used this street for picking up and dropping off passengers. As she slowed beside the bright wedge of light from the side door of the terminal, Runyan came flying out and dove head-first into the door she had reached across to fling open. As she goosed it away, Runyan looked back over his shoulder. Moyers had just turned into the far end of Howard.

Runyan turned back with a huge grin on his face. "Baby, we made it," he said.

CHAPTER 28

Louise and Runyan burst into her hotel room together, trying to beat one another to the king-size bed. They landed crosswise on it side-by-side in a dead heat and kicked off their shoes. Runyan chuckled into the bedspread, while Louise tried to snap her fingers. They seemed unable to make a sound.

"So much for Moyers," she said, trying again. Still no snap. They laughed as if this were inordinately funny.

Runyan, still chuckling, rolled over onto his back and stared at the ceiling, his hands interlocked beneath his head.

She said, "We bent him to our nefarious purposes—except I don't know what they are." She looked at him from the corners of her eyes. "What's our move—being reasonably young, devilishly attractive, and ridiculously wealthy?"

"We cash in the bearer bonds and give the money to Cardwell and his creep partners—thus becoming ridiculously unwealthy."

Louise swung around at right angles, also onto her back, so

she could rest her head on Runyan's belly and stare at the ceiling as he was. "Two out of three ain't bad." She remembered a vivid fragment of childhood: slumber parties, lying like this with her head on the stomach of her best girlfriend as they exchanged their innermost secrets. "I think I almost like it."

"Being unwealthy?"

"Not caring." She rolled her head to look up past the heavy rounded muscles of his chest to the strong line of his throat and thrust of his chin. "I came into this thinking you were just as rotten a bastard as . . . as the guy I was doing it for. And feeling that I was no better than either of you."

Runyan strained to look down at her, giving himself a momentary double chin. "But now you feel that you and I are better than that?" She nodded. He said, "Yeah, I like that, too."

Louise shifted around again, so she was lying beside him with her head cushioned on his shoulder. They stared solemnly at the ceiling, neither speaking for a long time.

"Just OUT isn't enough, is it?" Louise finally said.

"Not for me, not any more." After a long moment, he said, "There should be a ceiling fan up there, and this should be Singapore, or Tahiti, or Hong Kong. I keep feeling I want to *do* something—go mountain climbing around the world like that guy at Yosemite—"

"Giovanni."

"Yeah, him. Maybe a wilderness guide, or try to get a fishing boat . . . something that's . . . my own . . ."

Louise nodded. Both of them were relaxed, unpressured, the tension finally gone.

"I want to keep on writing," she said. "Keep at it until I learn how to make the words say on paper what I'm feeling inside. I keep catching myself thinking that the last five or six years never happened . . . or happened to someone else . . ."

"Seven or eight years," said Runyan in a sleepy voice. He gave a long sigh. "Down in L.A., when I charged Brother

Blood's car, I realized you always have two ways to run. Away from . . ."

"Or toward?" murmured Louise.

They fell asleep that way, side-by-side on the big bed in the dim room.

It was a little before ten a.m. when Louise pulled the Tercel up in front of the regional parole office. They had already returned their rented camping gear to the mountain shop.

"I'll check in with Sharples," said Runyan, opening his door, "make sure he doesn't have any excuse to call out the troops. Then we'll settle up with those guys and be home free."

"I'm still worried about Moyers—he's convinced you're going to turn the diamonds over to him eventually."

He squeezed her hand in reassurance and got out and closed his door. Louise drove down the block to an open space in front of a stucco-fronted meeting hall which once had been a church. She turned on the radio for company while waiting.

Runyan crossed the shabby waiting room to the desk where the angry-faced secretary was opening mail. The straight-backed, government-issue chairs that lined the walls were empty except for two bulky men at opposite corners of the room, as alike as Rosencrantz and Guildenstern, each reading one of the stale magazines from the dog-eared pile on the coffee table.

"Runyan. For Sharples."

The secretary looked up at him with almost frightened eyes. The bulky men, minus their magazines, converged on him from their opposing corners in a classic pincers movement. The closest one flashed an SFPD badge at Runyan.

"Inspectors Waterhouse and—"

"—Prince," finished the other, then added unnecessarily, "San Francisco Pee-Dee."

"We want to ask you a few questions," said Waterhouse.

"Downtown," said Prince.

"What about my rights?" asked Runyan. He fought down his panic reaction, kept his voice flat and his face unrevealing.

"We're not charging you with anything," said Waterhouse.

"Yet."

"Just asking questions."

"About Jim Cardwell's murder."

Runyan, shaken, demanded, "Jamie? Dead? How? When?" For years in San Quentin he had dreamed, schemed, wished for this moment; now that it had arrived, all he felt was shock, disorientation, and, strangely, a sense of loss.

"He does that good, don't he?" said Waterhouse.

"I think it's the way he moves his eyebrows." He added, to Runyan, "So since you ain't being charged with anything—"

"—Yet," said Waterhouse.

"You ain't got any rights."

"Yet," finished Waterhouse.

Louise was behind the wheel with her window rolled down, listening to the irrepressible Bruce Springsteen's gravelly voice explore his Jersey roots, when Moyers's hand came through the window to turn off the radio.

"Do I see diamonds in your eyes, my dear?" he said.

Louise, without even looking over at him, switched on Springsteen again. Moyers spoke over the sound of his voice.

"I ran a trace on you, lady."

Louise just managed to keep her eyes straight front. He *couldn't* have gotten past Vegas, could he? The trail *had* to dead-end there. Moyers reached in and shut off the radio again.

"I put a man in Vegas on you—it wasn't too tough." Though she still wasn't looking at him, she could almost feel him shrug. "It's always in the computers once you find a way in. So now I know who you *really* are. Where you went when you left Vegas. Why you're here."

Louise blurted out, "There aren't any . . ." but caught herself before the word "diamonds."

She sat motionless until she was in control again, then turned and looked at him. He was dressed in a brown suit with a blue shirt, a color combination she despised, one elbow on the frame of the open window.

"There aren't any reasons for you to tell him what you found out." Her voice was even. "I'm not in your way."

"Sheer enjoyment?" He said it as if he really was wondering; then he smiled unpleasantly. "You have to disappear, right now, totally. Right out of Runyan's life. I need him with nobody to lean on except me."

Louise thought she finally understood. Runyan had wanted Moyers in Yosemite so he would have to back up their contention that they'd actually been there the whole time. Moyers was just turning it around. Get her out of the picture, and only his word stood between Runyan and a return to prison.

"No," she said flatly. "I can't do that."

"I talk to him, you're not even a memory," said Moyers in an almost reasonable voice. "Whatever you want—him, the diamonds, peace in the world—you aren't going to get it anyway. Forget that. But go now, you walk away clean." He leaned closer; his face and voice were suddenly ugly. "Make me take him down, and I'll take you down with him. Accessory after the fact of murder for a start, then—"

"But he didn't kill anyone and I didn't—"

"Doesn't matter. It's what I can make the cops and the courts believe. And I can make them believe damned near anything I want. I've had a lot of practice, over the years."

She said quickly, desperately, "We could work together. I wouldn't keep you from recovering the diamonds. He'll . . . do anything I say . . ."

"Right now. Permanently."

She turned the full force of her emerald eyes on him, making sure that none of her meaning was obscure.

"I'd do anything you wanted, Moyers." She paused. "Anything."

He sighed; his obsessed eyes passed up and down her body, deliberately stripping her. With genuine regret he said, "God, I'd love to!" He shrugged. "But I can't take the chance. You're too dangerous. There's no way I could ever trust you, and I don't want to end up stupid about you like Runyan."

He stepped back and jerked a thumb. She wanted to fight; she wanted to keep on trying. But her will seemed numbed, paralyzed. If she could only talk with Runyan, he'd know how to . . .

But she *couldn't* talk with Runyan about her real past, not ever. She'd lost Runyan, as of this instant, and if Moyers told him everything, even the memory of her would be destroyed for him. After Yosemite, after Los Angeles, they both deserved more of the relationship than that; but Moyers's obsession with the diamonds went far beyond his lust for her, so she could never get to him the way she had to. She twisted the key, the engine roared, she fishtailed the car away with a shriek of rubber.

Runyan had been in a lot of interrogation rooms during his detention and arraignment and trial. They were all pretty much the same. Institutional pastel walls, wooden table with three or four straight-backed chairs with the varnish coming off them, a mirror which was, of course, one-way glass for those in the adjacent observation room. Built-in pickups going to a voice-activated tape recorder somewhere. Ashtrays on the table for those who smoked.

Runyan sat with his hands clasped in front of him, his elbows resting on the table edge. He had quit smoking his first week in Q, cold turkey, realizing that when you were inside, any addiction was a handle someone had on you. The overhead light brushed Waterhouse's pale elongated shadow back and forth across the table as he strode around.

He stopped and thrust his face down to within a few inches of Runyan's. "You drove back and shot him."

"I was half a mile up a mountain," said Runyan, not for just the first time. "With a witness."

"The same witness you say is your alibi for the Tenconi hit." He straightened up and sneered, "The same gun in both cases. And the maid puts you in Tenconi's penthouse just—"

"Leaving. Four hours before he got his ticket punched."

Waterhouse started pacing again, talking as if to himself.

"Eight years ago, Cardwell owes Tenconi a bundle. He's also night guard in a building where you just happen to pull a two-million-plus jewel heist. He shoots you. He's king for a day. They name margarines after him."

Runyan was silent. Waterhouse kept pacing.

"Tenconi is shot to death a few days after you get out of Q. Cardwell is shot to death a few days after that. And now our shiny new police computer discovers that you and Cardwell were old Army buddies—something nobody ever bothered to find out at the time of your trial. Suggestive, ain't it?"

Runyan said nothing. It was suggestive. If he'd been on their side of the table, he'd have been trying to make it fit into a pattern too.

Prince came in. He shut the door and leaned against the wall beside it with his arms folded. There was a sardonic look on his face. He gave a grunt of laughter.

"This Louise Graham must be the invisible woman."

Runyan, shaken, strove to hide it. He yawned and shrugged and wished he still smoked cigarettes. "Try her motel," he said. "She probably got tired of waiting in the car out there at—"

"Checked out," said Prince. "No forwarding."

Runyan felt all the animation leave his spirit. He felt the switches close, he felt the emotions drain away, he felt his face clench like a fist. When he turned toward them, he wore the mask he had brought out of San Quentin with him.

"Shame on me," he said softly in his flat prison voice.

CHAPTER 29

Runyan crossed the echoing lobby of the Hall of Justice from the elevator bank, pushed open the front door, and went out into the cool bright San Francisco day. On the steps he passed detainees' relatives coming from the bail brokers' offices across Bryant Street, chattering attorneys bright-voiced as magpies, plainclothes cops whose veiled arrogance made them unmistakable.

Waterhouse said behind him, "You got lucky, Runyan."

He turned, face cold and set. They must have been waiting since getting the news that Moyers had backed Runyan's statement concerning Cardwell's murder.

"For the moment," added Prince.

"Since the same gun was used, you're clean on both hits."

"For the moment," said Prince.

"It's bullshit, of course, but . . ." Waterhouse shrugged.

Runyan went down the steps without speaking. Louise had abandoned him again, obviously for good, which meant he was back to being an ex-con out on the street with a lot of people after him for one thing or another.

But he had one more job before resigning from the human race. Jamie was dead, and to his own amazement he couldn't just let it go. Maybe what the Chinese said was right: When you saved someone's life he was your responsibility forever. Delarty and/or Gatian, working singly or in tandem. Either way, he was going to take them down. He knew just how to do it.

At the East Bay Terminal, after making sure nobody was on his tail, he entered the same phone booth he had used after putting the bonds in the coin locker the night before.

When the phone rang Art was brooding out the window at the fine drizzle which was obliterating Portland's measly skyline. Win, lose, or draw, the fucking auditors were gone, anyway.

Gladyce stuck her head in the door. She'd had it in his lap every night for a week; pretty soon, he wasn't careful, she'd be going down on him under the desk. He'd taken to calling her Glad-Ass in their private moments.

"It's your brother on line three, Art."

He swung his swivel chair back to the desk, staring at her box and making kissing sounds with his lips as he punched line three. Gladyce giggled and pulled the door shut.

"Yeah, you in town, kid?" demanded Art into the phone.

Runyan's voice answered, "San Francisco. I just called to thank you for the loan, Art, and to tell you I'll be putting it into the mail to you this afternoon or tomorrow."

"Hey, bring it with you," said Art. Aggrieved, he added, "You aren't going to crap out on me, are you?"

"I'm sorry, Art, I won't be able to make it for a while. I'll be cleaning up some loose ends around here, then . . ."

Runyan had stuffed two sticks of gum into his mouth and started chewing them while talking with Art. When he hung up, the hand he'd rested casually on the moulding at the top of the phone booth brought down the coin locker key he'd stashed there.

He divided the bonds into two even packets: one he tossed back in the locker, feeding in a coin and removing the key again; the other packet he split to cram into the inside pockets of his jacket like a chipmunk stuffing nuts into its facial pouches.

Then he got a shoeshine at the stand beside the door to the men's room. As the black man daubed on polish and popped the cloth, head down and concentrating on the shoes, Runyan took the wad of gum from his mouth, wrapped the locker key in it, and stuck it against the inner edge of the front of the chair on which he was sitting.

It was the grassy interior of California here, hot and endless and unchanging, and Louise drove it half asleep. Far to the east was the blue smudge of the Sierra; to the west the low dark backs of the Coast Range. Here were just grass and moaning wind and hovering white-tailed kites, beautiful lean snowy birds that might have been gulls or terns except for that unmistakable predator's head.

What else could she have done except leave? If Moyers had told Runyan about her, any relationship between them was gone anyway. Better leave him thinking she was still working out some imagined debt to a former lover; he already had assimilated that incomplete part of the story.

Why was she not on her way to Hawaii or Florida or Puerto Rico or even Atlantic City, any resort area where a woman with her sort of talents could always find an uneasy living? Why was she returning to the house of a man she had come to loathe?

To pick up her half-completed scraps of stories, no other reason. From the beginning, she now saw, her brief season with Runyan had been doomed to failure—but it had somehow ruined her taste for the good life on the edge. His struggle to break free from his past had made her want to break free from hers.

Together, they might have done it. Apart, both would fail. But she was going to keep going through the motions, because conventional wisdom held that sometimes appearance became reality.

For the first time in over a year, she wished she had some coke. Coming back to Runyan, she hadn't brought her sleeping pills. She hadn't thought she'd need them. Without them, she needed some coke to kick her past this first, bad part. Well, maybe booze would do it. Maybe she would stop at a motel before dark, sign in, and get drunk.

Runyan sat on his side of the assistant bank manager's desk as the young middle-aged man with round glasses and a precise manner laid down the magnifying glass he'd been using to examine the sheaf of bonds, and cleared his throat. "I'm sorry to have been so ... cautious, Mr. Dawson, but these are worth a great deal of money, and as you come to me without references ..."

Runyan nodded pleasantly.

"I understand. But they *are* bearer bonds, and I am the bearer ..."

"Precisely," said the banker, as if the fact caused him pain. "And I realize the necessity of confidentiality in, ah, business arrangements which require a large amount of cash ..."

"Five-hundreds and a few hundreds are fine," said Runyan. "And a couple of envelopes to put them in ..."

Louise followed the freeway signs indicating FOOD—LODGING—GAS to the most anonymous motel in a motel row on the outskirts of Redding: motel, pool, restaurant, and piano bar all in one. She stopped in front of the office and put on her sunglasses to go register.

Runyan was waiting when Patty Cardwell came trudging

up with her blue book bag, dressed in another skirt and a white blouse, her sweater around her waist with the arms knotted in front. With her father so recently dead, he hadn't been sure she would come here to play; but he also figured she didn't have much of anywhere else to go. She stopped dead at sight of him, remembering. Then she came on.

"My daddy is dead," she said.

"I know. I'm sorry, Patty."

"He was shot." She sat down in a swing. "Like on TV."

He took one of the bank envelopes out of his inner coat pocket and crouched to stuff it down into her bag between schoolbooks. He looked up into her solemn watching eyes.

"I want you to go right home and give this to your mother. It's something your father gave me to keep for her. Can you remember that?"

She stared at him for a very long moment.

"Sure."

She turned and ran off with the book bag. Runyan watched her until she was out of sight. At least Betty and the kid would make out all right: The envelope contained just shy of $300,000.

Louise started with a shrimp cocktail, had a green salad with Roquefort dressing, went on to filet mignon with baked potato and sour cream and butter, garlic toast and the vegetable of the day—slightly undercooked zucchini—and finished with a chocolate mousse and two cups of coffee with cream and sugar. With the meal she had a half-carafe of Zinfandel. After the meal, she went into the lounge to drink Margaritas without salt.

Runyan taped the second envelope to the inside of one thigh with adhesive tape, had two cheeseburgers and a large fries at Jack-in-the-Box, then started drinking boilermakers through the Tenderloin. The coldness of his face, the flatness of his voice, and the obvious conditioning of his body protected him from the predators. They preferred their prey maimed; even at his most drunken, Runyan looked as ready to attack as they.

The night was a descending spiral into purgatorial images and impressions. Sometimes it was just faces. Faces lost, angry, sad, frightened, but always the faces of the Tenderloin: whores, male and female, beckoning and smirking, all ages, all colors, all races. Old people scuttling like crabs, their Social Security checks clutched in their pockets. Money went further here, and there was, after all, the illusion of life on these streets. Cops. Runaways. Dealers. Players. Narcs. People seeking action.

A degenerate youth, who could have been one of the trio he had used to get his stuff out of the Westward Ho-tel, groped him. He shoved the boy aside and shambled on.

A tough-faced cop paused to look him over, perhaps thinking paddy wagon and drunk tank. Runyan turned into a convenient corner grocery store and bought an apple, and the moment passed.

Later he was aware only of single sharp details: the line of a jaw; light shining amber through a raised drink; a heavy skull-and-crossbones ring on the finger of an outlaw cyclist; his own features distorted by a cheap back-bar mirror.

The streets seemed to grow darker; their detail softened from sharp to fuzzy to blurry and finally to contorted as his alcohol level rose. He threw up into the gutter between two parked cars, knowing he had to be finished with the Tenderloin's mean streets before they finished him. He would never escape if he gave in to the obscure feelings of worthlessness Louise's defection had triggered. Together, supporting one another, they could have made it. Alone, apart . . .

He drank hot black coffee and wandered again. The darkness became literal: The nighttime streets had become the black man's streets. He was standing in front of Sister Sally's. He started up the steps. He wasn't sober, but he was *compos mentis*.

• • •

The man was a foot taller and five years younger than Louise, with golden flowing hair, a bandito mustache, the bodybuilder's bunched shoulders and trim waist, and the self-centered stud's empty eyes. She had noted his bulging muscles at poolside, and had felt his eyes on her during dinner. For the past 20 minutes she had been feeling his hand on her thigh, and hadn't had enough self-esteem to remove it.

The woman playing the piano, who was pushing 40 hard enough to sprain a wrist, knew exactly. After ten minutes of dagger looks at Louise, she started to play the old *Pal Joey* tune, *The Lady Is a Tramp.*

Terrific. Everyone kept telling her, in words and actions, that that was who she was, what she was good at. So why fight it? It might as well be right away, like climbing back on the horse right after he'd thrown you. Otherwise maybe she'd never do it again.

"One more drink first," she said to the blond stud.

She paid. Of course.

CHAPTER 30

Voices, laughter, sweat, perfume, and smoke filled the air, all weaving through Donna Summer's *She Works Hard for the Money*. Runyan decided it probably was as apt a song for Sister Sally's as *He's a Sixty-Minute Man* had been for similar establishments in the post–World War II era of his father's bourbon memories.

Sister Sally, immense behind the bar, caught Runyan's eye but made no move to serve him. Instead, she leaned across the bar toward him, her great breasts overflowing against the polished hardwood. Her hair gleamed with pomade like shavings of gunmetal.

"Somebody made his point the hard way with Taps last night. Firebombed the mortuary and caught up with him at home. Now they gonna be playin' *Taps* at *his* funeral." She gave a sudden rich peal of laughter that shook the mounds of her breasts and belly like bagged jello under the tentlike *futa*. "Gonna have to bury him out of somebody else's funeral home."

A petite shapely girl with knowing eyes and very full lips, wearing only a red Fleur de Lace bodysuit of filmy silk, slipped up beside Runyan. She twined her arm through his.

Feeling a sad stillness inside him, he ignored her to say, "His woman? Grace?"

Sister Sally shrugged, disinterested in any women not her own. The girl pulled Runyan toward the stairs to the second floor with professional urgency.

"C'mon, sweetie," she said, "Emmy Lou show you some grace."

Louise unlocked the door of her motel room and went in, the blond stud close behind her, already breathing hard as if mere proximity put him in rut. Before she could even close the door he had her pressed back against the wall, his face buried in her throat, his practiced hands cupping her breasts, massaging them, seeking the nipples through the cloth of her brassiere.

For a few moments she submitted, head back against the doorframe, eyes shut, trying to will participation. But when his groping hand hiked up the front of her skirt and slid down the front of her panties, she made a strangled sound in her throat and tore free, her eyes wide open, wild as the eyes of a fire-trapped horse.

"Look, I made a mistake," she said. "I'm sorry, I really am. I just . . ." She sought words to describe an inner devastation for which there were no words. "Just . . . sorry . . ."

He chuckled and began forcing her to her knees. "I dealt with prick-teasers before, little lady. Once you taste the—"

She rammed her head violently up under his chin, hearing his teeth crunch together and knocking him just enough off balance so she could shove him out the door. In the same motion she slammed and locked it.

He began pounding on it, shaking it against the frame with the violence of his blows. As she slid on the night lock, he began yelling obscenities; from somewhere down the line of units came another male voice, heavy as a baying hound.

"KNOCK IT OFF OR I'M COMING OUT THERE AND YOU WON'T LIKE WHAT I DO WHEN I GET THERE!"

The pounding ceased. The obscenities ceased. Louise, her head against the door, heard mutters, then retreating steps. Back to the lounge to soften up the piano player; still plenty of time. The night was yet young.

But Louise wasn't. She got her suitcase out of the closet and began putting back into it the things she had taken out. Much better to drive all through the night than this degradation. Which, come to think of it, had never seemed degrading before. Perhaps she had begun building a soul.

Runyan lay on his back on the bed, enveloped by Emmy Lou's cheap musk, staring at the ceiling and remembering the last time he had lain like this, with Louise, as they had talked about their hopes and plans. Gone, all gone.

Emmy Lou, hunched between his legs, was crooning to it like a mother comforting a frightened child.

"Don't you fret none, honey, you jus' a little tired. Emmy Lou jus' work on you a little more, bring you up proud as—"

Runyan raised his head to look down at her small, ebony body crouched over his dead stick.

"I'm sorry, Emmy Lou," he said. "I made a mistake. This was the wrong way to say goodbye to someone."

Ten minutes later he was standing in front of the empty firebombed shell of Taps's funeral parlor, hands in pockets, thoughts somber. When he got Taps involved in their old San Quentin fantasy, he should have remembered that Taps wanted it all, right now, and could be a fool in the things he would do to get it. Just like Jamie, he had ended up with nothing. Not even his life.

There was the stench of scorched electrical wiring in the air, the reek of released chemicals, the thick char of wood ash and oily blistered smell of bubbled paint. Police CRIME SCENE tapes were up, but there seemed to be no watchman on duty. He stepped over the plastic tape and moved through the ruins of the building toward the rear.

Grace sat behind her debris-littered desk in what was left of the office, the only illumination that of streetlights through the glassless windows. Disorienting shadow patterns were cast by the remains of thin metal decorator blinds hanging at grotesque heat-twisted angles.

As she poured herself another shot, Runyan came through the doorway, glass crunching loudly beneath his soles. Grace tossed back her drink and poured again.

"I guess I loved that rotten ugly nigger," she said. Her voice sharpened. "Where's that little lady of yours? Only good thing about you."

"Gone." Runyan picked up the phone receiver from the floor, replaced it on the hooks, then lifted it again and listened. There was a dial tone. He tapped out a number. "She found out there wasn't any free lunch."

"Huh-uh. No way. Not that lady. She left, somethin' drove her off." She looked at him again. "You, probably. God knows you bad enough news."

Runyan, listening to the phone ring, picked up her whiskey, toasted her slightly with it, and tossed it back neat. He set the shotglass down in front of her again.

"Bad enough news," Grace repeated softly.

"Hello," said the phone almost cautiously in Runyan's ear. He said, "Gatian? Runyan. Cardwell convinced me. What you want is in a coin locker at the Trailways Depot."

Grace was saying to herself, "Guess I should leave."

"The key is under the right-hand chair at the shoe-shine stand. I called you because I figure you don't have the balls to cross Delarty."

Grace sighed, "Guess I got nowhere to go."

Runyan added, "I don't want either one of you clowns coming at me afterwards, claiming that I stiffed you."

Grace said, "Guess I got nothing to go with."

"Wait," said Gatian, "I don't underst—"

"This squares us," said Runyan, and hung up.

Grace was watching him. She gave a bitter little laugh. "Getting yo'self off the hook?"

Runyan didn't answer. He was tapping out another number on the phone. As it started to ring, he took the other banker's envelope from his pocket and tossed it on the desk.

"Police Emergency, Operator Four," said the phone.

Grace, frowning, reached out a slow hand for the envelope. Runyan said to the police dispatcher, "Tell Waterhouse to get his butt over to the Trailways Depot right now if he wants to close out the Tenconi and Cardwell hits."

He hung up. Grace had the packet open and was riffling through the money with unbelieving fingers. She raised her head to look at him. "Runyan, I can't take this. All along Taps was planning to double-cross you."

"You weren't," said Runyan.

Austin was a narrow one-block alley which ran behind Runyan's rooming house on Bush Street. As Runyan came trudging up from Franklin, the man standing on the roof of the building across the alley moved quickly back from the edge so he wouldn't be seen.

The man went back down the narrow stairway to the second floor. The building smelled of Oriental cooking. He unlocked his door, crossed the room without turning on the lights, and crouched in front of the window. It looked directly at the back of Runyan's rooming house. He settled in to wait.

Runyan stopped just inside the doorway, hand still on the light switch. The room had been expertly tossed by someone who didn't care if he left tracks. The mattress had been slit and gutted, the pillow was a spent storm of feathers, the mouldings had been ripped from the baseboard.

Runyan came the rest of the way into the room, shut the door, and started to take off his shirt. The closet door opened and Moyers stepped out, a flashlight in his left hand, his right hand in his topcoat pocket. He had a nasty-sly grin on his face.

In that instant, Grace's remark of an hour before returned—if Louise had left, someone had driven her off. His manner said Moyers was the one.

A great weight lifted. His mind began to work again. He tossed his shirt on top of the bureau, went to the sink, and ran cold water to splash over his head, face, shoulders, and chest.

"Find anything interesting?"

"So you didn't stash them here. You can't blame me for making sure." When Runyan didn't respond, he added, "She really got to you, didn't she?"

Runyan gave a harsh little laugh and turned off the water and started rubbing vigorously at his hair and face with a towel from the rack beside the sink. Louise had been forced away. What else mattered?

Well, staying alive, for openers.

He said, "You wanted her gone to isolate me so I had nobody to back up my story except you. But I can't figure what you threatened her with to make her go."

He crossed the room, still rubbing at his hair, and tossed the wet towel over the back of the room's single straight-backed chair. He put his foot on the seat and leaned one elbow on the raised knee.

Moyers said, "You don't want to know. Just give me the diamonds and I'll be on my way."

"I'll bet you will," said Runyan, "since you never intended to turn them back to the insurance company anyway. First you nudge the authorities into granting me a parole, then you furnish me with an alibi for two murders. If I don't hand them over, you withdraw the alibi and I go back to prison." He laughed harshly. A lot of things had fallen into place for him. "But if I *do* hand them over, I get killed."

Moyers was standing with his legs slightly spread, square on to Runyan, both hands now in the topcoat pockets. Runyan's left hand had retained its grip on a corner of the towel, where Moyers could not see it.

"I can arrange police protection against—"

"Who? Delarty and Gatian?" Runyan shook his head. "Hell, it was you killed Tenconi and Cardwell—to eliminate some of the competition. So giving me an alibi gave you one, too. The beauty of it is that I give you the diamonds, I get shot, and Delarty and Gatian get blamed for it. Getting revenge for their dead associates. Neat."

He tightened his grip on the towel.

"But Delarty and Gatian got arrested about an hour ago for trafficking in hot bonds. And there aren't any diamonds. When I went back to get them, they were gone. So you see—"

Moyers was jerking the silenced .38 from his topcoat pocket, but Runyan had already snapped the towel. Moyers yelled as the wet cloth bit at his eyes. He staggered back against the window shade, firing two wild shots as he did.

The shade shredded as the window burst inward with the double-crump of the 12-gauge shotgun across the alley. Moyers was blown across the room, his back a pulped mass. His inert form slid face-first down the wall to settle in a heap against the torn-up baseboard.

CHAPTER 31

The intense glare of the spotlights inside Runyan's room cast an almost palpable bar of white light through the open doorway, washing the wallpaper flowers from the opposite wall. Policemen moved in and out, their shadows cast almost black by the relentless spots. Runyan stood in the hall beside the door, head lowered and arms folded on his chest, listening to his landlady's quiet hysterics from the living room downstairs.

He thought he had it figured out now. Of those who had known about the diamonds, only Louise's former lover was still unaccounted for. And the shotgun blasts which had killed Moyers had unmasked him. The problem was, what could he do about it? What *should* he do about it? Stay here? Leave? Seek vengeance? Seek Louise? Or give up everything, slip back into the narrow existence of so many ex-cons who let their past fuck-ups forever dictate the shape of their futures?

Prince emerged from the room carrying a clear plastic evidence bag with Moyers's silenced .38 inside it. At almost the exact moment, as if they were indeed identical twins, Waterhouse appeared at the head of the stairs. He waited while two green-coated ambulance men edged their way out of the room and down the stairs with Moyers's bodybagged corpse, then they converged on Runyan like a nickel defense on a quarterback.

"Here we got a thirty-eight automatic with a commercially made, expansion-chamber type silencer," said Prince. He held up the evidence bag as if it were a trout he had caught. "Moyers had the fucking permit for the piece in his pocket—though not for the silencer, of course—and a current passport and a one-way ticket to Israel. Obviously planned to kill Runyan and keep the diamonds for himself. Diamonds Runyan ain't got anything to say about."

Runyan remained silent.

Waterhouse asked, "What about across the alley?"

"Ah, yes. Across the alley. Real cute over there. Guy rented the room today. Big and bearded. The lab boys are going over it for prints, but it doesn't look as if he even whizzed in the john. Just waited. We also got two twelve-gauge double-oh shell casings." He looked at Runyan and laughed sardonically. "Looks like somebody tried for you and got Moyers instead."

Waterhouse nodded. "It figures. 'Cause after our anonymous phone tip we find Delarty and Gatian just getting a packet out of a locker at the bus station. Do we find diamonds inside?" He answered himself. "We do not. We find seven-hundred K in bearer bonds so hot the bank in New Orleans don't even know they're missing from the vault until I call them up and tell them. Still had the bank's bands on them."

"If I had a dirty mind," said Prince to Runyan, "I'd think you fenced the diamonds, bought some hot bonds somewhere—probably the same fence, and he's a guy I'd like to meet—and then set these guys up with some of the hot bonds for a fall because they blew away your old pal Cardwell."

"Would you care if I did?" asked Runyan.

"Hell, no! I'd love it. Because if you did or not they *think* you set them up with the bonds, and they're *pissed*. Since there doesn't seem to be any way we can touch you legally, the idea of people out there after you suits me just fine."

"To say nothing of how pissed our shotgunner's gonna be when he finds out he scragged the wrong guy," put in Prince with a sort of dreadful relish.

"So we think you ought to leave town," said Waterhouse. "Like maybe today? Like maybe far away? We'll square it with Sharples down at the parole authority. He sounds so cooperative I keep thinking you must have something on him, too."

Runyan kept silent.

Prince said, "By God, another one would like your ass! Go die in somebody else's jurisdiction, Runyan."

"So Waterhouse and Prince don't get stuck with the paperwork," said Waterhouse.

Maybe they were right, Runyan thought. Maybe it was time to leave. Maybe it was time to go home.

Portland had changed in 12 years, had grown, become citified, gotten cluttered up with traffic—but still, despite the new skyline and the Portland Mall, reminding him in some odd way of suburban Cincinnati on a bad day. It was still too early to make contact with Art at the truckers' union office, but he wanted to see the old homestead first anyway, alone.

He caught a Woodstock 19 bus and rode it out past Reed College to the end of the line at 103rd Street. Old white frame houses almost touching elbows on barren, tough-looking streets. Fast-food joints next to liquor stores, pickups with gun racks, outlaw motorcyclists in black leather, semis snoring through gears on the thruways. Not much really changed.

A mile's walk brought him to his old high school. He went up the walk to the front entrance of the tan three-story stone building. It was not yet seven o'clock in the morning, so it was still locked up tight.

He pressed his nose against the glass, cupping his hands

around his eyes so he could peer in. The hall stretched straight ahead through the building. Classrooms had their doors still open from the cleaning people the night before.

Runyan seemed to hear the muted rattle of football cleats on the terrazzo floor, vague youthful voices, laughter. It was almost as if he could see padded and suited football players coming up the hall from the far door, backlit almost to transparent silhouette. They were carrying their helmets in their hands or under one arm. He and Art were among them, chatting and laughing as they headed for the locker room after practice.

He turned away and went back down the walk to the sidewalk, filled with an unfocused yearning that was neither regret nor nostalgia. Rather, a sense of incompletion.

Ten minutes later a teen-ager in a pickup truck stopped for his raised thumb. The boy had an acned chin and a spiky yellow cellophaned Laurie Anderson haircut, but he talked of the hunting season with the reverence usually reserved for religious beliefs. The inevitable gun rack held an 1897 Winchester 30-30 lever-action carbine, the old one with the hexagonal barrel.

"That takes me back," said Runyan, sounding momentarily old even to himself. "I killed my first buck with one of those old Winchesters."

"Me too," said the boy. "Last fall. First one." His warm brown eyes shone at the memory. "Me'n my dad . . ."

The pickup dropped him and rattled off along the country blacktop. Runyan started across a stubble field toward low hills covered with hardwoods, oaks, and elms and a few birch, not yet leafed. Twenty minutes later, memory bursting upon him, he swerved to a brush pile and kicked it.

A cottontail bounced out, jinking away in terrified delight, and in his memory Runyan raised the long-barreled .22 Colt Woodsman and snapped off a single shot. The rabbit tumbled over, throwing up a spray of snow. Today's rabbit zipped under another brushpile and was gone.

Runyan went on into the marshy triangle at the foot of the hill. When he stepped on a tussock of winter-dried grass, a hen pheasant burst out in a rush of wings to angle up and away like the ringneck 15 years before, in full plumage, long tail fluttering and stubby pheasant wings beating to raise his heavy gallinaceous body. Runyan raised the .22 and fired a single shot. The pheasant took a heart-stopping pinwheel tumble to land a hundred feet away with an audible thud. The hen set her wings and glided into safe cover in the hedgerow at the far edge of the marsh.

Runyan nodded slightly to himself, then went on. Ten minutes later he came out of the woods to the narrow drive meandering up through the hardwoods. Now he strolled uphill as then he had walked up the slight rise in the cemetery to the open grave. He'd been in hunting clothes and had carried the fresh-shot rabbit and pheasant. Snow had fallen from a leaden sky.

The other mourners had departed but the casket was still above the open grave on its slings. Runyan laid the rabbit and the pheasant on top of it, disturbing the snow as little as possible. The blood, fur, and bright feathers were very vivid against the white. He stood with his bared head lowered.

Goodbye, Pops. Goodbye to deer-shining out of season in the hardwood belt across the creek. Goodbye to jump-shooting mallards down in the river bottoms. Goodbye to woodsmoke and mellow bourbon by firelight and all the things that made a part of you mine. The part they could never get at.

A long time ago, almost in another life; a life of primary colors which had long since faded. Then he thought of Louise, and wondered if his losses were more in memory than in fact. Only time would tell.

He rounded the final bend at the edge of the trees and got his first glimpse of the old-fashioned white two-story frame house set in among the oaks. He went up the turn-around, past the kennels where memory foxhounds bayed and wagged their tails and leaped around the young Runyan and

Pops in hunting clothes and cradling cased shotguns in the crooks of their arms.

Runyan turned away. The kennels were empty and weed-grown, the dog houses half rotted away. So were the bird feeders in front of the house, though he almost heard the clamor of the chickadees and juncoes as Pops put out a mesh bag of suet and ten pounds of cracked corn.

The doors were locked, so he continued on around the house to the corner downspout that once had been his nocturnal route to adventure. It seemed as sturdy as ever; he started up, jamming stiffened fingers into the space between the spout and the siding, his body angled out from the wall.

At the second-floor level, he reached over and pushed up the unlocked window of what had been his folks' room. He swung himself from the drainpipe right in through the window, landed off-balance on a rag rug, slid across the polished hardwood floor and crashed into a table by the far window. A typewriter fell into his lap as a snow of papers blizzarded in all directions.

Runyan sat on the floor and laughed. "Watch that first step, it's a bitch," he said aloud.

The room was essentially unchanged. Same old faded family portraits on the walls, his mother's old-fashioned tortoise-shell toilet articles on the dresser top, the double bed with the brass bedstead and the quilt his mother had made . . .

He remembered his father dying in that bed, his arm hanging limply over the edge, smoke from his cigarette running up to the ceiling in a thin unwavering blue line. That arm, unable to hold a cigarette up in the air, gave Runyan the same wrench as finding a good foxhound that had gotten mixed up with a bobcat.

Runyan righted the table and put the typewriter back. He had just collected the scattered papers when he heard cars coming up the drive. More than one of them. He folded the papers over and stuffed them almost absently into his pocket.

Through the front window he watched a current Caddy

stop at the foot of the front walk. Art got out. Runyan's lips twitched. Trust Art to drive the biggest, gaudiest thing Detroit currently produced.

As a woman got out of the second car, Runyan crossed to the door and stepped out. A complex of conflicting emotions made his inner compass spin. From below drifted up the sound of the front door opening distantly, the woman's voice demanding sarcastically, "What's the matter, Art, did you think I was going to sneak out here and steal the silver or something?"

Runyan opened the door of the study and went in, shutting off the voices and sounds from below.

CHAPTER 32

I don't understand you any more, Louise," Art said coldly. "You fucking got what you went after, why did you come back?"

He was in the middle of the front room, between her and the stairs. It was an old-fashioned room with an overstuffed leather couch and chairs of rosewood and needlepoint seats. On one wall was *The Dying Indian* hunched on his pony, feet hanging, head drooping, warlance angled down in defeat.

Louise, reeling with fatigue, knew just how he felt. Despairing. She had driven all night, had stopped off at Art's office to tell him she was going out to the house for just a minute, and now this.

"I came to get my stories, Art," she said in a tired voice. "My typewriter. Small things, but my own. So if you'd just kindly get to hell out of the way . . ."

Art, his face ugly with emotion, said, "Why bother? Now you can buy a thousand fucking typewriters." He added bitterly, "How much did you work him for, baby?"

She stared at him, astonished.

"Is that what this is all about? I told you on the telephone, I just wanted—"

"Oh, don't give me that shit, Louise. When you called me that last time, I knew he was getting the diamonds and you were getting a share. You saw your chance and took it. I don't blame you. But you knew I really needed that money to pay off the union pension fund before the audit. Shit, they're going to indict me! How could you—"

"Art . . ." Then she paused. What was the use? He wouldn't believe whatever she told him anyway. Maybe she should just turn around and walk away.

Up in his father's den, Runyan was walking slowly around, touching things, looking at things, remembering. He could almost see Pops and him across the big hardwood desk from each other, feet up, sipping bourbon.

Remember, boy, you can do things you can't walk away from.

Maybe he was doing one now. He moved past the desk to the glass-fronted gun cabinet. It was unlocked, as it always had been: No one in this house had ever been careless around guns, there'd been no need for locks or safety devices.

After a hesitation more mental than physical, Runyan opened the cabinet and reached in and took out a leather case. He carried it over to the desk, unzipped it, and almost ritualistically brought out the two halves of a broken-down 12-gauge double-barrelled shotgun. Someone had crudely sawed off the barrels to make them several inches shorter than legal length.

That removed the last doubt, although he'd already been morally certain. Who else still alive and free had known about his Bush Street address where the second shotgun attack had taken place?

He snapped the two halves of the shotgun together, then broke it at the breech to expose the chambers, laid it down on the desk, and went back to the cabinet to bring back a box of

12-gauge double-oh shells. About half the shells were missing. He took out two of them. Stood with them in his hand, thoughts, memories, and emotions running through his head.

The sound of raised voices from downstairs dimly penetrated the thick floor of the room. He started slightly, dragged back from his reverie.

"Goddammit, Art, let go of me!"

She had tried to leave, but he had grabbed her from behind and spun her around. He started kissing her, smearing his face against hers, seeking her tongue with his. His mouth smelled of the cigars he smoked.

'C'mon, baby, one last go for old times' sake . . .''

She twisted and raged and broke free, face flushed with anger and effort. "Jesus," she exclaimed, "to think I ever—"

Art backhanded her across the face, a full-arm vicious swipe that knocked her right to her knees. She stayed there a moment, as a fighter who has been knocked down will stay there for the mandatory eight-count.

Then she picked herself up, warily—frightened more of his thoughts than of anything else. He believed Runyan had gotten the diamonds and that she had gotten part of the action. If he tried to extract her nonexistent share from her . . . But as he bulked over her threateningly, there was only sarcasm in her voice.

"Terrific! Hold that pose! This is just the way I want to remember you!"

Art said in a low enraged voice, "Sure, you'll fuck my brother any time he'll have you, but since I don't have a stash of diamonds to hold you . . ." He burst out, "You were there because I sent you, for Chrissake! You never heard of the diamonds until . . ."

He stopped because she had started to laugh: genuine, delighted peals of laughter.

"Everybody has been after the diamonds ever since Runyan

got out of prison," she said. "But someone built a subdivision over them. The diamonds don't exist any more."

Even as she said it, she regretted it. No telling what sort of rage that would arouse in him. Art had never been long on ironies. But to her amazement, he started to guffaw, his heavy laughter so delighted there could almost have been an edge of hysteria in it.

"You're taking it well," she said flatly.

"No, the joke . . . the joke's on you. And on Runyan." He laughed again. "The fucker's dead."

Louise felt herself stagger, almost fall, as if he had struck her again so swiftly and unexpectedly that she did not feel the blow, only its aftereffects.

"What are you telling me?" she exclaimed. "*Goddamn you, what are you saying to me?*"

"That he killed me," said Runyan's voice. "With this shotgun."

They whirled toward him. He was standing at the foot of the stairs, cradling the cocked and ready sawed-off shotgun in the crook of his left arm.

Art, ashen-faced, began backing away, hands raised to shoulder-height. He tried a sickly smile.

"Hey, Runyan, look, I can explain . . ."

Louise felt dead, frozen inside. Now Runyan knew it all: about her and Art. That it was his brother who had schemed to take the diamonds from him. She had let Moyers drive her away for nothing. She should have stayed, let him do his worst. Now it was too late. Now there was too much that was bitter between them to ever . . .

But she didn't understand, either, what Runyan had said. That Art was the shotgunner who had tried to *murder* him?

"Twice," said Runyan. "The first time was straight economics—he thought I was dumb enough to be running around with the diamonds on me. He called you off so you wouldn't know. But he missed, so he had to send you back in." He turned to Art with a sardonic smile. "The second time you shot the wrong guy."

Art had backed slowly away across the room until he touched the credenza against the far wall.

"He . . . he knew the Bush Street address," said Louise haltingly. "That's where he sent me the second time . . ."

"He sent me money there." He turned back to Art. "But *why* the second time, Art?" He asked it as if he really wanted to know. "Why, when you thought I'd already recovered the diamonds and they were out of your reach anyway? Was it just simple frustration? Doesn't seem much of a reason to kill someone."

"He needed the money to stay out of jail," said Louise.

Even as she spoke, she knew there was more to it than that. So did Runyan. He advanced on Art as if stirred to anger by his own recital of the facts.

"Or was it because of Louise?"

In his own way, she knew, Art had loved her. To lose her to his younger brother after a lifetime of . . .

Runyan slightly raised the cocked shotgun, then the tension seemed to go out of him. He set it down on the dining table without even bothering to uncock it.

"To hell with it." To Louise, he said, "I just came back hoping to find you here anyway. And maybe to say goodbye to the old place. I've said it. So let's go."

The final weight of guilt lifted from her spirit. They knew everything about each other now—and neither of them cared. It was just what he had said: The world had started turning when the two of them had come together.

He put his arm around her shoulder and turned her toward the front door. Behind them, ignored, Art started to inch toward the forgotten shotgun.

"I want to go to Vegas and be an exotic dancer," Runyan said. "Ostrich feathers and mesh stockings and bare boobs . . ."

They both started to laugh, almost to the front door. Behind them, Art leaped forward and snatched up the already cocked shotgun. Runyan turned, half-laughing.

"You aren't going to do anything with that, Art. It's over. We've all lost out on the diamonds. It's all over."

But Art panted disjointedly, "You broke in . . . shot her . . . I struggled with you . . . got the gun away . . . shot you . . ."

"Don't be a fool, Art," he said. "You saved my life when you shot Moyers. You didn't mean to, but you did. So you go your way, we'll go ours—"

Louise thrust herself forward. "Art, for God's sake—"

"In the back, through the window shade, that's your style," said Runyan. "You don't have the balls for this, Art."

For answer, Art jerked both triggers of the shotgun at point-blank range. As Louise cringed back with a shriek, eyes squeezed tight shut, the hammers fell on empty chambers. She opened her eyes, stunned. Runyan was standing there just looking at Art almost sadly.

"I didn't think you really would do it, Art," he said. "Not face-to-face like this. For no reason at all." He turned away. "But just in case, I didn't put any shells in it."

Runyan slid in behind the wheel of the Toyota. Louise was rummaging in her purse for the keys, her actions almost frenzied.

"You don't understand," she exclaimed, "he hates you, he's always hated you."

She handed him the keys. Runyan inserted one into the ignition with maddening deliberation. "He just used up all his hate. Even if they do indict him, his lawyers'll—"

"You still don't understand. He's capable of anything. This isn't just for the diamonds, or the indictment that somehow he blames you for, or even the fact that you have me and he doesn't. You played a dirty trick on him when he was just three years old, and he's never forgiven you."

Runyan shrugged as he started the engine. When Art was three? What difference could it make now? He took off the handbrake and put it in drive. Above and behind them, one of the bedroom windows burst outward as Art rammed the stock of a 30.06 deer rifle through the glass. He reversed the weapon, threw it to his shoulder, fired just as Runyan started around the far end of the traffic circle. A starred hole appeared in the rear window at the same instant they heard the thud of the rifle.

"*Holy shit!*" yelled Runyan. "He *does* hate me!"

He goosed it, the car fishtailing out of the turn-around as a second slug creased the hood. Then they were into cover as the road went down through the sheltering hardwoods. Runyan wiped his face with his hand, but tried to be casual when he spoke.

"He always was a lousy shot." It came out tense and excited. All of a sudden he wanted desperately to know.

"What trick?" he asked Louise.

"What?" She was emerging from under the seat slowly, like a turtle unfolding from its shell when the danger has passed.

"When he was three years old. What trick did I play—"

"Oh. You were born."

For a moment Runyan stared at her blankly, then he started to laugh. They were running out across the flat at the foot of the hill. By looking back, Louise would be able to get a last glimpse of the house. She started to turn, but Runyan put a hand up against the side of her face like a horse's blinder, blocking her view. He gently turned her face forward again.

"You want to be turned to a pillar of salt?" he asked.

She stared at him hard for a moment, suddenly solemn, then nodded slowly in agreement. As he turned into the main road, she sighed.

"I never did get my stories."

Runyan, with a flourish, pulled her folded stories from the inner pocket of his jacket and handed them to her. She grabbed them with a little exclamation; but then she just sat there with them clutched almost absently in her hands as he drove them away from there.

Sat there and wondered if she was going to cry and wondered if she felt this way out of sadness or out of joy. Then she thought, Maybe this is the way it always is with endings. And with beginnings.

a **pear** falls

to the ground...